Tell Us About The Olden Days, Please Mommy

.....as I recall

Phyllis R Brandow

Order this book online at www.trafford.com
or email orders@trafford.com

Most Trafford titles are also available at major online book retailers.

Printed in Victoria, BC, Canada.

ISBN: 978-1-4269-1456-0

Our mission is to efficiently provide the world's finest, most comprehensive book publishing service, enabling every author to experience success. To find out how to publish your book, your way, and have it available worldwide, visit us online at www.trafford.com

Trafford rev. 11/25/2009

www.trafford.com

North America & international
toll-free: 1 888 232 4444 (USA & Canada)
phone: 250 383 6864 • fax: 812 355 4082

TO MY GRANDCHILDREN

This collection of stories is written for my grandchildren Shyanne and Jaydon Ulrich and all the little Brandows as they arrive. I hope they will always remember that their Grrrammy Bear was a fun person with a huge sense of adventure and a great sense of humor. A special person in their lives who loved nothing more than to seek out a wild and crazy adventure, to unravel a mystery, to laugh out loud and have lots of fun.

ACKNOWLEDGEMENTS

It is written with thanks to my own children Ryan Brandow and Tasha Ulrich, who from a very young age, crept into my bed at night begging me to tell them about the olden days. They could never get their fill. They helped me put together many details of their stories and encouraged me to have the stories published.

With thanks also to my siblings Eleanor Panaschuk, Beatrice Tudor and Josephine Kyryliuk who quibble endlessly about the accuracy of my memory "as I recall" the events of my life.

A huge thank you to my dear friend Barbara Tootell, my English grammar and punctuation specialist, who proof read this work many times with lots of love and red ink.

A special thank you and a big bear hug to my granddaughter Shyanne Ulrich who lovingly volunteered to create the cover for this work using only her love of the stories and her ten year old imagination. Thanks also to Todd, her daddy, for his technical support.

And finally many thanks to Vona Priest. As my Psychiatrist and my good friend, Vona led me through the floor plan exercise of every home I ever lived in. Writing down all the details that came to my mind about these homes was cathartic and soul-cleansing for me. This exercise restored many wonderful memories and it helped me come to terms with some of the tough memories of my life back to early childhood. The exercise spawned an interest in preserving the memories for posterity.

This collection of stories is my gift to God created using His gifts to me.

INTRODUCTION

By the age of 20 years I had moved almost that many times, which included staying in one location for a full five years. My life became one adventure after another. I learned to make the most of every situation that I found myself in and have as much fun as possible because I knew that I wouldn't be there very long. It was hard for me to make friends. Before a relationship could be established I was moving again. I knew a lot of people in my travels but we were never anywhere long enough to form the bonds required by me, for true friendship. I spent most of my time alone or with Josie, my little sister.

Born in a small mining town on the Ontario/Manitoba border, which was devoured by a wildfire soon after, I lived most of my childhood in Manitoba, moving frequently to where my parents could find work. Even when it became my decision to stay or to move I chose to move. I didn't know how to stay. Staying is not something we did as a family.

I went from my birth place in Central Patricia, Ontario to Manitoba, where I spent my childhood in Kamarno, Inwood, Teulon, Selkirk, Transcona and Winnipeg. As a young adult I moved to Edmonton and The Lower Mainland where my children were born in Vancouver, on to North Vancouver, North Delta and Surrey. I moved to Calgary for fourteen years while raising my children, then back to One Hundred and Fifty Mile House near Williams Lake, BC. I returned to Alberta and my current home in Airdrie, AB when I became a Grammy.

While living at One Hundred and Fifty Mile House and after a death in the family, I realized how far off track my life had gone. At that time, I chose to make changes in my life. I decided to get to know Jesus once again. All of my life I did feel God's presence even though I was walking in darkness. I could name a million times (possible exaggeration) when He would rescue me, protect me, guide me, lead me, warn me, comfort me, teach me and love me through it all during those dark years. The stories in these pages represent some of those times.

Finally in 2000, I packed up the Fifty and moved back to my family in Calgary to embark on the ultimate adventure of grandchildren. The process had already begun. I was a Grammy and didn't want to miss another moment of it.

I am very grateful for every detail of my life good and bad, every person that ever crossed my path and touched my life positively or negatively. I am grateful for every choice I ever had to make and every decision I made over this half century of life. These are the combination of events and life experience that have shaped me and brought me to where I am today.

All of these stories are true. They are written as I recall them.

CONTENTS

Part Two-LIFE WITH CHILDREN

Part Three–THERE IS LIFE AFTER CHILDREN

150 Mile House, BC

PART ONE

MY CHILDHOOD

SCHOOL DAYS

How I wanted to go to school! I was infatuated by the school uniform. Each day I watched as my older sisters dressed in their beautiful uniform, which consisted of a pleated navy tunic with a cloth belt, over a white blouse and a navy tie, as they went off to school. Everyone going to school looked alike. I thought they looked marvelous and I so wanted to be one of them. I would and did do anything I could to go to school, sometimes with success.

The first time I ever went to school I was not old enough; I may have been four or five years old at that time. I followed my older sisters to that beautiful old schoolhouse. The teacher, who taught both classes, let me stay for a while if I promised to be a good little girl.

The schoolhouse was a two-room building with a large dark foyer. The foyer had no windows. There were coat hooks on all the walls because this space doubled as the coat and boot room. One of the big bright rooms housed the grades six to twelve students. The other room held all the elementary grades.

The elementary classroom, the only one I ever entered, was very large. It held all grade one to grade five. There were many windows on one side of the classroom. Blackboards covered the opposite wall and the front of the room behind the teacher's desk. Chalk and erasers could be found in the ledges beneath. The floors were oiled-wood. A wood burning space heater stood to one side near the front of the room. To a child with a good imagination, this heater looked like a short man with a pot belly. There were piles of wood on either side of the stove, carried in by the daily monitors. Student seating consisted of several rows of wrought iron/wooden desks, some single, others double. The desks were in neat rows. They were screwed on to two by four's to provide easy moving for floor cleaning.

There was one extra desk in this classroom. It was one side of a double desk. I was permitted to sit in this desk when the teacher allowed me to stay. Whenever she left the room to tend to the high school students the older elementary kids would ask me to do things that I didn't know were wrong. These kids told me to draw on the blackboard; sometimes they asked me to erase the blackboard. I always complied because I wanted them to like me. They were all at school and I wanted to be with them. The teacher would be upset; she would be disappointed in me and have to send me home.

I recall one such occasion where I was getting ready to go home before everyone else. The teacher gently took me by the hand and walked with me to open the door. She liked me and she was kind to me. She helped me with my sweater and commented on the lovely Mother's Bouquet I was wearing. A Mother's Bouquet is a long string of shiny safety pins of various sizes attached one to another hanging on a mother's shirt. My Mother's Bouquet was hanging on my dress from my neck to my knees. As I wandered home alone I wondered if I would ever be old enough to go to school and wear the beautiful uniform and stay in school all day.

At last I was six and old enough to go to elementary school in grade one. By now we had moved to Teulon, Manitoba and the school was not the same; it was bigger and much more an institution. How excited I was to wear my very own amazing school uniform. I was one of the school kids now; I was so very proud. No one could ever stop me from going to school now. I would study and practice and learn and I would be the smartest kid in school. I would never be without the school uniform now because I had older sisters and I knew that meant hand-me-downs.

How shocked and saddened I was when I entered grade three. To my horror and utter disbelief the beautiful school uniform was being discontinued. I wouldn't be stopped though. I continued to wear my uniform including the hand me downs until they were completely worn out. Rags! Now I had to start wearing my own clothing. It wasn't long until I realized how shabby my clothing was as compared to that of my friend Sandra. Sandra M. wore her new tartan kilt with a long-sleeved white blouse and a matching tartan scarf. Every day she seemed to have something new while I wore my same faded shirt and worn out pants. She was still my friend but I didn't feel equal anymore. School soon lost its charm and appeal and I lost my heart for school when the uniform was discontinued.

I loved to go to school and school was wonderful, especially my uniform. Everyone looked alike. There was no economic class distinction among the students. In grade three all that changed and what a terrible blow it was to my ego to know that now I would never be able to measure up. I was poor and though it was not my fault, it did not change my status. I wasn't the same as everyone else anymore. I was poor and now without the school uniform that fact was painfully obvious to everyone. I was treated differently. To fade into the background and be sure no one would notice me, I found myself cheating to lose. Now I went to school only because it was the law. For years after, even to the end of my school life, I mourned the beautiful school uniform and the glorious memories it held for me.

FROM THE WINDOW

I may have been eight years old when Dr. Goodwin's wife died. I didn't really know Mrs. Goodwin; I hadn't seen her more than a couple of times. Perhaps she was ill all the time we were neighbors. I didn't know what "die" meant even though my own daddy had recently died. I did know, however, that those people were never seen again; I just didn't understand why. Children were never allowed to ask questions about death. Children could be seen but not heard. Soon after the death all of the earthly possessions were disposed of.

Josie and I were sitting in the window of the playhouse in the woods next door. It was our refuge. In this playhouse we talked about the things we didn't understand. We wondered about daddy and Mrs. Goodwin and what really happened to them. What is dying? What does it mean? Where did our daddy go? No one talked about death openly; it seemed very mysterious and very frightening for a kid with a wild imagination.

The playhouse was located in a wooded area at the back of the property behind the neighbor's workshop. It was along our property line where the Ferley and Goodwin acreage's met ours. It was a cool spot under the trees in the heat of a summer day. We spent a lot of time there with our baby dolls and our big lady purses. We prepared scrumptious meals of mud pies and dandelion salad for our ravenous imaginary families. We always served dessert which we picked directly from Mrs. Ferley's fruit trees, without her permission I might add. Our imaginary families weren't fond of fresh fruit so we usually ate it for them.

With all that space, why did the good Doctor choose to put his garbage pile under the tree right across the fence from our playhouse? As we sat on the windowsill of the playhouse chatting as we often did, the scent from the garbage pile wafted toward us and it filled the air. The scent was that of cosmetics. Oh my gosh! Oh-my-gosh! The Doctor was throwing out his late wife's personal effects now that she was deceased. Slowly our eyes scanned the garbage pile. There were heaps of little boxes, bottles, bags and tubes of all sizes. There was clothing, shoes and handbags. Uh Oh! Run for your life! There are false teeth in the garbage pile!

Mrs. Goodwin must have left in a terrible hurry that she left her false teeth behind. Those teeth kept me away from the playhouse for the remainder of that summer; they were also the source of many a nightmare. I wouldn't have been more afraid if the playhouse were haunted.

I may have been eight years old when Mrs. Goodwin passed away. I didn't really understand anything about death. I only knew for sure that those people were never seen again and after it happened, all their earthly possessions were disposed of, including their false teeth.

DOWN MEMORY LANE

This was the favorite home of my childhood. I spent five years of my life here from age five through age ten. This is the longest period of time that I ever lived anywhere while growing up. I remember the details like I was still there: the fence, yard, house, garden, woodpile, outhouse, barn and the bees.

The four-foot fence was once fancy crimped wire to be envied. It stretched across the property in front of the trees, the caragana hedge and the lilacs. This same fancy wire fence continued down one side of the acreage nearest the house from the sidewalk out front to the chicken coop out back. The gates were of the same fancy wire on metal frames. A well-used gate in the back led to the neighbors' yard and the wonderful playhouse. A gate in the front yard to the north opened into our yard and the wooden sidewalk.

The sidewalk was old; the wood was worn and damp even in the heat of the sun. Some areas were rotting. There were boards broken in the middle from use and age. Bright green moss grew in the cool dark places on the underside. I can still smell the moist decaying wood. The wooden sidewalk divided the perfectly manicured front lawn.

The lawn was neatly mowed with a razor-sharp push mower. The edges were carefully trimmed by hand; the flower gardens were tidied to perfection. This outside job was one of my favorite chores. I carried water from the neighbor's well four doors away to water the flowers. The rock garden is where mom's prize-winning dahlias grew amongst a profusion of other colorful flowers. The garden was immaculate! No weed would dare poke its head through the moist black soil in such a carefully protected environment. The robins would rather risk starving their young than to chance being caught removing an earthworm from this cherished garden. The north verandah, which bordered the garden, was a cool place to escape the heat of summer.

The house was wrapped on three sides by a twelve-foot deep verandah. To the east, the verandah was completely enclosed by a half wall with screen above and a screen door at the front. This was the protected place for children to play during inclement weather. Sometimes we even thought we would sleep out there although we never did conjure up that kind of courage. Virginia Creeper entwined itself in the wire mesh and grew to the roof. In summer it was like a wall as it kept the area well shaded and cool. That well established Virginia Creeper was home to a robin family and many other birds. To the west the verandah was open.

An old sofa and a couple of equally old comfortable chairs were located in front of the dining room window. We often sat out there on a warm evening. The large residence across the street was a home for rural boys while attending school in the great metropolis of Teulon. Mom worked there. The boys from that residence came by in the evening with table scraps for our chickens and tall tales for us little girls. Sometimes we snuggled together as one on the old sofa during a violent thunderstorm to watch the inevitable Manitoba lightning show. Of course there was the test of courage which meant that we had to sit quietly during the storm, no whining or crying.

Outside the west door is where is where the milkman left the milk that he delivered. We would find the cream popping out of the freezing milk bottle in winter. This door opened to the living room. There were two large north-facing windows in the living room. It always seemed dark and cool in there in the summer. An old wind-up gramophone stood between daddy's rocking chair and the door. In the center of the long room stood a tall potbellied coal-burning space heater, which kept the room toasty in winter. Mom's bed, which doubled as a sofa, was against the farthest wall. A door divided the living room from the kitchen/dining room, the other half of the main floor level.

One long window in the kitchen faced south to the garden; the other faced west to the neighbors. A heavy round oak table sat in front of the large cast iron cook stove. The stove had a warming oven on top and a hot water reservoir beyond the oven. Those two large items dominated the room. Near the west window sat a big worn comfortable red chair. Under the stairs was the cool enclosed storage place for all the preserves. There were plums, Saskatoon's, blueberries, crabapples, cranberry sauce or colenna as we called it, jams, jellies, pickles, vegetables, venison and chicken. The stairs leading to the upper level made their exit from the southeast corner of the kitchen. A tall old-fashioned radio with its many useless yet decorative knobs stood near the stairs.

There was an addition built on to the house. In winter the addition was storage, boot room and freezer. There was a large rain barrel there that was filled with snow to be melted and used for laundry and bathing during the winter. This barrel was filled whenever it snowed to ensure we always had water. In winter we had an old Coca Cola cooler that we used as an outdoor freezer for the chickens.

From spring to fall, the cast iron cook stove with its coveted water reservoir and warming oven was moved outdoors. This was to prevent the house from getting too hot during that unmerciful summer heat of Manitoba. The addition became a summer kitchen of sorts. Here all the canning preparation was done. Everything from cleaning the berries we had gathered to plucking and cadavering the chickens we had slaughtered.

From the kitchen the stairs led to the second level. The first three steps at the bottom and the top three steps wrapped around the corners. The rest of the solid steps went straight up. We often sat at the top landing chewing on our toenails and chattering as we tried to avoid *BEDXYZ*, mom's unique way of spelling bedtime. There was a window at the upper landing. I recall how Jack Frost would beautifully decorate that window for us in the winter. As we scurried up the stairs to bed we would reach up and put our hot little fingers on the icy window to change the patterns. By morning, Jack Frost always cleaned up our mess with a beautiful new design.

Often we would sneak out of bed, tiptoeing to the bottom steps, to listen to scary stories on the radio when mother thought we were sleeping. She liked to listen to *The Shadow* and *Adventures by Morgue* two very scary stories that came on the radio in the late evening hours. We had to sit very quietly however scared we were to hear how the story ended. Sometimes hearing the ending was equally as scary as not hearing the ending. I'm sure that some of my many nightmares came from the bottom steps to spend the night with me in our bedroom.

Upstairs there were three bedrooms. The first one was Ellie's bedroom; it was small fitting only a double bed. I spent hours in that room on the floor in front of the closet untangling the wool used to knit her Mexican sweater. The second bedroom was also small. This room had a double bed and a dresser but this one was never used. In this room we three little girls sat on the bed by the window singing in the evening. The third bedroom was very large. It was larger than the other two bedrooms and the hallway combined. This room and its double bed were shared by us three little girls.

Did you count the bathrooms? There were zero actual bathrooms in the house; however, we were not hard done by. We had a slop pail by night which we girls took turns carrying out to dump at the out house every morning. By day the two seat outhouse with it's collection of catalogues accommodated us well.

On the ceiling of that big room was the entrance to "the attic." In my sleep I climbed a six-foot ladder, removed the cover and went up into that attic. My big sister Ellie rescued me. She brought me safely down the ladder step by step and put me back to bed still sleeping. The attic is the hiding place where I believed my nightmares spent their days while they waited to visit me again at night. There were two large south-facing windows in this bedroom.

Through the bedroom windows we could step out onto the roof of the summer kitchen. What a great place for stargazing or telling scary stories in the dark! The pitch of the roof was ever so slight and we had no fear of falling off. In dreams I often did fall, jump or fly off the roof always waking up just in time to save myself. At the lower right side of the roof was a giant rain barrel.

The barrel was on the ground and was almost the height of the roof. When the rain barrel was full it became our private swimming pool. We put the six-foot log ladder into the barrel so we could easily get out and back up on the roof. Usually the rainwater was used for bathing or laundry, but in summer it was also our pool. I remember being in the barrel and seeing millions (possible exaggeration) of mosquito larva sharing the pool with me. For me that was pretty much the end of the fandango private swimming pool. I spent much more time in the huge five acre yard.

Plum and crabapple trees hid in the wooded area at the side of the house. In spring these trees were visible, they were beautiful and fragrant; in fall they were heavy laden with ripening fruit. I remember tasting the fruit often at every stage of the ripening process from pucker sour to sweet and juicy. A tall oak tree in that wooded area towered above everything else. A lower limb was home to a long rope swing with a wooden seat. We kids thought we could survey the entire world if we could just pump high enough. We would often swing in pairs, one sitting the other standing both pumping with all our might. Perhaps today we'd see the entire world. Beyond the oak tree a lush vegetable garden grew.

The vegetable garden contained row upon row of thriving vegetables that awaited the rain and the sun in their turn. The garden seemed to get larger every year. Copious jars of canning came from this garden, pickles, vegetables and relishes. Sunflowers grew seven or eight feet tall. I was little so I may remember big. I recall how in autumn the thick fibrous stocks of the sunflower plants had a spike punched through them as they were transformed into stilts for the neighborhood kids. Near the garden was an ongoing pile of sawdust.

This pile of sawdust was years old. This is where we four girls cut firewood for the winter and often during the winter. Two girls on the buck saw, the other two holding the long logs and neatly piling the wood. A worn-out sawhorse, the only four legged creature we ever owned, stood in the center of the sawdust pile. Each piece of wood was laid on the saw horse, measured and cut to an exact length, then neatly piled. The ends of the woodpile were woven to ensure a neat secure pile along the fence between the back door and the shed.

Half of the shed was used for storage of the razor sharp push lawn mower, canning supplies, coal oil and lanterns, the cast iron bath tub used for jar washing in canning season and many other miscellaneous items. The other half of the shed was the chicken coop. This was where we fed the chickens in summer so they could feed us in winter. The chickens slept in the shed at night but by day they ran around in the wire run built just for them. Sometimes we let them run in the yard. They laid their eggs in the nesting boxes provided before they were let out.

We had electricity but not indoor plumbing. There was an outhouse beyond the chicken coop. The outside of the small structure was weathered wood. A half moon was cut high up in the door. A hook and eye latch held the door shut on the inside, while on the outside the lock was a simple piece of wood nailed onto the building. The inside boasted two holes, a large hole for the adults and a small hole for the children. Between the two seats sat a pile of old Sears and Eaton's catalogues used for reading or wiping as the situation dictated. On the floor sat a bag of lye with a scoop in it. There was an unwritten outhouse rule that no one dare forget. *If its pee let it be, if it's brown pour it down.* Outhouses were kept fresh by using lye to decompose the daily deposits and it worked well.

Past the outhouse was the path we used when carrying drinking water by the pail from the Rhone's well four doors away. Beyond the path was the barn. The inside of the barn is not clear in my memory. The barn was not really used for anything; first it was too far from the house and of course our only four-legged creature was a sawhorse. The corral in front of the barn was the storage place for the hay cut from our field by the farmer. Most activity at the barn was on the roof from which we jumped into the hay below until we were caught and got into trouble with the farmer.

In the middle of the field, about barn distance from the house were stacks of curious white boxes! They were stacked about five boxes high and there were several stacks. We learned the hard way that these boxes were beehives. We learned that bees lived and worked in the hives. We learned the hard way what they did for us or to us if we got in their way. We also learned why mom forbade us to go near them. I especially recall the poor mans first aid for bee stings. A pail of water was thrown into the garden and we were thrown in after it. It was a mud bath that mom claimed would take away the pain of a bee stings. Supposedly it worked but I won't vouch for the technique. I preferred our usual, always on hand first aid, which was to pretend nothing had happened

The balance of the five acres was hay field. The hay grew tall; it was taller than a child between the ages of five and ten years! At least two times in a season a farmer would come by with his horse-drawn mower to cut the hay. He would come by later with a horse-drawn rake. The hay would then be stooked by hand to dry, then stored in the corral until needed. Burning the hay field in spring was a way of warming the ground early to ensure that second crop of hay.

In spring my mom was transformed into the community pyromaniac. She loved to burn the hay field. It was her happiest time. She was never prepared though because she had such great confidence in her grass burning skills and techniques. Every year the fire would get out of control and we kids would have to run in all directions for help.

Yes indeed, this was the favorite home of my childhood. It tops the memory list as the most exciting five years of my childhood. Those details, how vividly they stand out in my mind, from the house to the barn and everything between.

THE PLAGUE

Often I had dreams as a child. Some of the dreams were not only very frightening but also recurring. They were not the sort of dreams that I'd wake up from and instantly forget; which was inevitably the case with great dreams. I'm not sure how I would know that as I had only ever had nightmares. My dreams were the kind that remained in my mind all day long. The instant my eyes were shut again, whatever the time of day, the dream would return. I don't suppose that either listening to scary stories on the radio late at night or letting my wild and vivid imagination run away with me ever helped me to sleep any better at night.

I was terrified of the dead. I didn't really know anything about the dead or even what it meant and perhaps that intensified my fear. Although my dreams were always frightening, I could be or do anything I wanted in them. I could also open my eyes and keep them open to temporarily end anything too frightening.

As this particular dream began a terrible plague was spreading through our small town. It could be seen! It looked like a green mist. I watched as it touched people and they would become very sick. Soon there were so many sick people in the town there was hardly anyone left to take care of them. People were dying at a startling rate and they had to be carried away to the morgue. Although I didn't know what the morgue was, I did know that it was full to overflowing with the dead. I heard people talking about it. Bodies were now taken directly to the cemetery for burial. My older sister and I were among the many bodies laid out at the cemetery.

The cemetery was a beautiful place with lush green grass. Some tall oak trees shaded areas of the cemetery which was enclosed by a tall hedge, an ornate iron fence and a tall gate. With so many people gathered there milling around the dead, it was difficult to appreciate the beauty of the place. Although dead, I could still hear, see and talk.

I was telling my sister how afraid I was about being buried alone, especially in the ground. She was quiet, yet I knew that she was listening to me. I went on to tell her that I wanted to be buried with her. I knew that she would be pleased not being buried alone. My sister didn't answer me. She had her eyes closed and that frightened me. Now I needed my mom!

She was coming to see us. I could see her head above the surrounding hedge even before she entered the big wrought iron gate. She had worked hard all day and she was walking slowly. I waved franticly and called out when I saw her. She glanced up, but there were so many dead bodies there on the ground that she couldn't see us. I waited for her to come closer. I was crying hard by the time she arrived at our plot. I told her how afraid I was about being buried alone. I told her that I wanted to be buried with my sister in the same grave and in even the same coffin. Mother said very matter-of-factly, "Well, we'll see when the Coffin Man comes!"

Mom looked around the cemetery at all the deceased she knew and she knew most of them. She wandered away as she looked them over and chatted with the survivors. The Coffin Man was coming now; everyone looked up to see him at the gate. Under his arms he carried two small coffins just the right size for my sister and I and he walked directly towards us. I awoke from my dream singing *Rudolph the Red Nosed Reindeer.* At seven years old it was the only song I found to be appropriate for such a terrifying dream.

I had escaped the dream this time, however it was destined to recur many, many times over the next forty plus years. The details never changed, yet they frightened me as much or more than the first time I dreamed it.

RUDOLPH THE RED NOSED REINDEER

It was the year that my daddy died, so I was five years old when we moved to that big old house in Teulon; the one with the verandah around three sides. We had five acres to play in. The entire property screamed adventure. How fortunate that we all had the Tudor sense of adventure which we inherited from our mother.

On a warm summer evening Josie, Beaty and I would sit in the upstairs bedroom window of that big old house singing to any passer-by that cared to listen to us. We sang *Evening Shadows Make Me Blue, Let Me Call You Sweetheart, How Much Is That Doggie in the Window* and all the top songs of the late forties and early fifties. Sometimes we would practice church hymns as we were often called upon to sing in church.

In this huge old house we three little girls slept together in one big sagging bed in the largest upstairs bedroom. I was a very insecure child so I liked to sleep with my sisters; I can't say the same for them. We slept in turns, two at one end and one at the other end of the bed to allow enough space to sleep comfortably. Because I felt so insecure and unsafe, I liked to sleep in the middle. Sometimes we'd snuggle together like little kittens; someone would always wake up with numb arms or legs.

I had dreams and nightmares almost every night. Often I dreamed of being chased and being unable to run. I never did get caught though because it was my dream and I'd wake up just in time to save myself. I'd sing my favorite happy song, *Rudolph the Red Nosed Reindeer* and sometimes I could go back to sleep.

This night was much like all other nights. As I slept, one of my sisters rolled on my leg causing it to become numb. I was dreaming that a huge rat had eaten off a large part of my foot! Even sleeping, I knew it was a bad dream; yet I couldn't resist raising my foot to my hand so I could feel the foot to be sure. To my horror I could feel the foot with my hand but I couldn't feel the hand with my foot. It was like touching someone else's foot. Something was very wrong and now I was wide-awake. I knew that it had to be my foot because it was at the end of my very own leg but why couldn't I feel it? I was afraid to turn on the light in case I really didn't have a foot. Worse yet, what if the rat was still there?

I lay awake a long time singing *Rudolph the Red Nosed Reindeer*. I watched the ever-changing shadows dance on the wall where the moonlight entered the dark room, while my vivid over-active imagination ran out of control.

Slowly the foot began to tingle. It hurt as the feeling returned to that lower limb, yet I was happy to feel the pain. It meant I did still have a foot and the rat really had been just one in a long line of terrifying dreams.

THE OLD HOSPITAL

We lived in Teulon, a small town in Manitoba, where the General Hospital was our neighbor to the right. It was a huge three-storey building with a full basement. The hospital was painted white with green trim. Large trees and bush, including a scruffy hedge that acted as a fence, surrounded the building. There were very wide, steep, wooden steps that led to the front doors. The fire escape was a sheet metal slide from the second floor to the ground. Inside, the walls were stucco-covered laths and the floors were beautifully polished hardwood. An auction sale on that warm spring day symbolized the end of an era as the old hospital was vacated, emptied of its contents and over the summer carefully dismantled.

As a child I suffered tonsillitis regularly. Our neighbor on the other side, Dr. Goodwin determined that I would need to have my tonsils removed. Mother made an appointment for me to have this procedure done at once. On the appointed day all the little Tudor girls holding hands climbed over the fence, through the hedge and walked up that steep wide staircase leading to the front doors of the hospital. We entered the building brave and excited! We all had our tonsils removed that same day; I clearly remember the sore throat, the many popsicles and the ice cream.

A short time later all the patients were transferred to the new hospital a few blocks away. An auction sale was held at the site of the old hospital, where everything of any value was sold to the highest bidder. Every person in our town was there. Mother purchased a hospital bed on which the head rolled up. We three little girls fought over that bed all hoping it could be our very own. The hospital was then closed forever.

Soon after, workmen arrived to dismantle the entire building piece by piece. We were forbidden at this time to go near the old hospital because it was dangerous to be in the way of the workmen. This motherly caution not only demanded rebellion but served to make the idea of being there that much more appealing.

The fire escape of the old hospital, a slide, attracted the attention of all the neighborhood children. It was built with sheet metal about four feet wide, which made it very hot or cold depending on weather. It started at the balcony of the second floor window and ended on the ground behind the hospital. What kid could resist such a slide? This became the play area of choice for many town children; the place where we could most often be found. We had a lot of fun on that slide with all the other kids. The only itsy bitsy problem encountered on the slide was a three-corner tear in the sheet metal about halfway down. We children were aware of the problem tear and we would carefully lift one cheek as we whizzed on past it. The only injury incurred on the slide was to the odd pair of pants.

There was a locked window at the top of the slide by the landing. We children all realized that in the event of a fire patients on the third floor would have to walk the stairs to the second floor before climbing out of the window to the slide and down to safety. We spent a lot of time peering in through that window to the vacant room beyond the glass. The window at the top of the slide aroused the curiosity of all the children. What could be beyond the glass and through that open door? It wasn't long until the window was "accidentally" broken and now with the window out of the way a whole new set of adventures could begin.

At any given time many children could be heard echoing through the empty rooms and hallways on every level of the old hospital. The workmen didn't stop us as they carried out the demolition work. They warned us of the dangers then kept on working.

Slowly over the summer the building began to shrink, the roof, the third floor, second floor and soon there was nothing left except the floor on the main level. Amazingly, no one had ever been seriously hurt. The workmen started to remove the flooring on the main level plank by plank. Josie and I wandered over to peruse the site and perhaps offer the workers some expert guidance. We noticed that the joists beneath the floor were now visible. We seized this opportunity to show off our balancing skills as we gingerly stepped out on those joists. As we gained confidence, like everything else that we did together, it became a competition. Josie and I were now running on the joists and laughing. Again the workmen reminded us that we shouldn't be there because it was dangerous; again they didn't insist we leave.

I was running behind Josie when, uh oh, the joist under my foot gave way. Minutes later I was waking up in the basement in a pile of nail-infested laths which were once an integral part of a stucco wall. A nail had gone deep into my hand and it hurt. A workman collected me from the basement, removed the nail from my hand and started to carry me home. I begged him to put me down. I couldn't let my mother see that I'd been hurt after her many threats and warnings. The workmen set me down near the fence which I promptly scrambled over.

At home I immediately wrapped a towel around my hand so that mother couldn't see the puncture mark from the nail. How could one talk about the accident that happened on forbidden territory. No, it had to remain unspoken. Appearing to be playing a game with the towel on my hand, I quietly administered the only first aid available in our home which was to pretend it hadn't happened.

Our neighbor to the right was no more. The steep wide steps leading to the front door and the most exciting metal fire escape were gone. The fine stucco walls and beautiful hardwood floors were in the past. The auction sale symbolized the end of an era. The hospital was vacated, emptied of its contents and dismantled one piece at a time. Only the memory remains of a summer filled with adventure and heavy danger as we lived on the edge at the old hospital.

THE HEAVY DOOR

In 1952, as a seven-year-old child, my sisters and I would go to the babysitter's house after school while mom was at work. Most often we'd walk along the railroad tracks until we got to the babysitter's road. In our lunch boxes we collected grain for our chickens as we walked past the tall grain elevator.

This particular day Josie and I walked along the main street which paralleled the railroad tracks. We shop-looked the store windows as we walked. On the corner we were approaching stood a small white building with a huge door and no windows anywhere on it. It was always locked. No one would ever tell us what was in the building. It was a mystery and nothing excited us more than unraveling a mystery. We tried the door of that little building every single time we walked by. We often went out of our way to walk by as we did that day.

Knowing that the exceptionally wide door would be locked again, we tried it anyway. We pooled our strength and pulled on that door together. It took every bit of our combined strength, but this time we gained entry and the heavy door "slammed" shut behind us. It seemed dark as our eyes adjusted to the change in the light.

Inside, the little building was dimly lit as though by candles. Heavy purple velvet curtains swaged to one side divided the room. Behind the curtain we could see a beautiful carved wooden box with an open lid. It was sitting on a table. We knew instantly that we had found the greatest treasure ever. We hurried over, climbed up on the table and prepared to claim our major treasure.

Uh oh! This is not our treasure and why is this old lady sleeping here in our treasure box anyway? Uh oh! We didn't know what was wrong but we knew something was. Jumping down, we ran for the door. We were overcome by an inexplicable sense of urgency to be out of there. What a big heavy door! It was hard enough to pull open when we entered but now it seemed even heavier to push and hold open while we made our hasty exit. We'd have to tell Mrs. Mullen (the babysitter) about this adventure.

We ran all the way to her house as fast as we could go. Breathlessly we told her all about the little white house without windows and the lady sleeping in the box. To our utter astonishment Mrs. Mullen didn't seem a bit surprised by our story. "That's my friend Gracie," she told us; "Gracie died and is gone to Heaven now to be with God." "No she isn't," we protested, "She's sleeping in the fancy treasure box on the table in that little white building on the corner." It took a while but Mrs. Mullen managed to calm us down. She gave us a silver St. Christopher medal (the patron saint of travelers) and asked us to lay it on Gracie's chest as we passed by there on the way home. We agreed to do it, but only because she was the adult, she was the sitter and she had a big son.

We played, had snacks and gave no thought to our earlier adventure until it was getting dark and we were ready to go home. We reluctantly took the silver medal and promised to lay it on Gracie's chest as Mrs. Mullen requested.

We realized now that we had been alone in the same room as a dead body. What in the world could that mean? We were afraid and had no one to answer the many questions on our minds.

We knew that funerals were most often held in the family home. We had seen caskets open for viewing through the living room windows or on a verandah as we passed by.

As we walked closer to this building which we now knew was the funeral home, we became hesitant. "I really don't want to go back there, do you? Well, I know we said that we would but I'm too scared. Aren't you scared? I don't even want to walk past there. Let's go home the other way." The closer we came to the little white building the more determined we were to just avoid it and lie if questioned. By the time we got to the railroad tracks we could see the little building. It could have been neon and calling our names it was so obvious to us now in the darkness. Our minds were made up! Never again would we go into that building. We quickly dug a hole in the cinder stones and buried the silver medal right there under the railroad tracks. Hopefully the patron saint of travelers would protect the train passengers because it would certainly do nothing for Gracie.

Our curiosity about the little white building with the big heavy door and no windows was now well satisfied and we would never again go near it. In future we'd walk along the railroad tracks to the babysitter's house, we'd gather grain for our chickens as we passed by the elevator and we would try very hard to mind our own business.

THREE FINGER JACK

At ten years old we moved from the favorite home of my childhood to the equally small town of Selkirk, MB. We lived across the tracks in a small house that mom called a shanty.

Josie is my younger sister, nine years old. She is left-handed and blind in her left eye. Most often she could be seen with her left hand covering her left eye and her right hand behind her back.

Josie and I played together most of the time. These days we were into playing doctor as we were that particular day. We were given a huge long cardboard box to play with. The box immediately became our hospital bed. In our game we pretended that the patient had a contagious disease and we could only touch them with a very long stick. Josie was lying in the box while I played the doctor. I walked around the box and poked at her with my long stick as I made my diagnosis.

From the neighbors upstairs window we could hear the top song of the day blaring from the record player. We began singing along with the record. *I found my thrill, on Blueberry Hill.* As we played our game and sang we could hear the neighbor's tractor motor start up. That sound brought both of us to attention. Our game was over for now.

This neighbor, Mr. Shepard, had a tractor with a buzz saw on the back which he used to earn his living cutting firewood for people. He often took us along for company or to help. We wondered if he was going to cut wood for someone. We both wanted to go with him so we hustled over to find out. He said that he was going to cut wood and that we could both go but we had to have shoes on.

We both wanted to go with him so we hurried to find our shoes. It seemed that in the summer our shoes were always lost; we only needed them to go to Sunday school or to go cut wood. Josie found hers first and she ran over to the neighbors without me. I searched for mine but they were nowhere to be found. I heard the tractor pull away without me.

I cried as the tractor, with Josie aboard, disappeared down the road. I was upset that I didn't get to go but I was even more upset that Josie didn't help me find my shoes. My bosom buddy dared to go without me. How could she! I busied myself trying hard not to dwell on this rejection as I searched for a fun game for one. A few hours later my game for one was interrupted by a knock at the door.

Mr. Shepard was at our door; Josie was not with him. He was looking for mom. I asked him why he needed mom and where was Josie? He told me that there had been an accident and Josie was now in the hospital. Josie had been balancing on a smooth round log. As usual, she had her left hand over her left eye and her right hand behind her back. When Josie lost her balance on the log she reached out with her right hand to save herself from falling and grabbed the spinning saw blade. Josie lost her little finger, her ring finger along with half of her hand to that saw. I was horrified to think that we had been playing doctor and now my little sister was in need of a real doctor.

Josie was in the hospital for about ten days and in a thick plaster cast for weeks. She had seventy-two stitches to repair the damage. This was prior to the days of micro-surgery, of saving the digits and having them sewn back on. Josie would have to live the rest of her life missing those two fingers. Her physical therapy to regain the use of that hand went on for months.

I often accompanied Josie to the hospital when she went for physical therapy. It got us out of school at least one hour early. One strengthening exercise that we both liked was dipping her hand into the hot wax. She dipped it again and again allowing a bit of cooling time in between until there were many wax layers on her hand. Once it was all cooled she had to bend her fingers cracking the wax to remove it. The layers increased with the regained strength.

The therapist often allowed me to do this exercise with Josie to keep her company and of course it became a competition between us. Sometimes we'd dip our hands so many times that there would be no wax left in the container and our hands could barely be lifted. We weren't able to remove the wax by moving our fingers but needed to pull it off with our free hand. When therapy was finished we cleaned up. At Jose's urging we then went to look for the plastic skeleton, which we thought was real, in the classroom down the hallway. Hopefully before it got dark outside and with our minds filled with fright, we'd start the long walk home.

Kids can be very mean. Kids in large numbers are just plain cruel. When Josie came to school after the accident everyone wanted to see her hand. Some kids called her "three finger Jack." Although I'm sure that it hurt her to hear that, she just laughed along with them, she never complained. Now, fifty years later no one even notices that hand.

MENTAL ANGUISH

I was about twelve years old when my oldest sister Ellie started working at the Selkirk Mental Hospital. She was a nurse's aide and she got to wear a uniform, a crisp white apron over a pink dress and a stiff white nurse's cap. These uniforms were laundered at the hospital. They were then taken home and used as required over the next week. Each week the uniforms were returned to the hospital for laundering and a fresh lot for the coming week was picked up. I was afraid of the patients I saw at the mental hospital and I worried about Ellie's being there, although I thought she was very brave to go.

Ellie had a very good memory for what she needed to do in a day but occasionally she was in too big a hurry. Sometimes she would forget to take her laundry in on laundry day or she would forget her eye glasses. If we younger girls saw either of these items lying about, we would leave the house immediately for the whole day. Ellie would surely phone home to beg us to bring them to her. I personally couldn't bear to leave the phone ringing. What if it was one of my friends? Because of my vanity I was often conned into the delivery task with promises of money and special favors.

I'd have to make a trip to the Mental Hospital, then inside where all those patients were. I may have to wait alone in the dark foyer, with those patients around me, while someone looked for Ellie.

I was terrified to go near the Mental Hospital, even to walk on the opposite side of the road, as Ellie was well aware. I knew that my mind would be working overtime; I was bound to have nightmares for weeks to come but the promises of money and special favors sounded too good to pass up.

FOOD FOR THE FAMILY

The small town where I lived as a child was the location of the Mental Hospital. My oldest sister Ellie worked at that hospital as a nurse's aide. It was a huge complex with many tall brick or stone buildings: there were baseball diamonds and expansive grounds and gardens. There was also a farm that fed all the residents and occupied many of them.

Sometimes the town siren would ring out and all the mothers would gather their young children and run for the safety of their homes. The siren meant that one of the potentially dangerous patients could not be found on the grounds and it was a warning to stay indoors until the patient had been found or returned to the complex. As children we were always on our guard. The mental hospital held many a mystery for us because it was not talked about openly, only in snickers and whispers much like the morgue.

I was afraid to go anywhere near that hospital and I usually kept a good distance away. Josie was my very brave younger sister. She was thirteen months my junior and not afraid of the Mental Hospital or anything else. Together Josie and I experienced many a grand adventure in which there was always the test of bravery. To prove bravery it was necessary to perform any feat chosen by the other; however cruel and unusual it may be, it must be carried out with no fuss and no tears. If one failed the whole town would know of the cowardice, the other would see to that.

Because she knew I was terrified, my mean little sister usually had me walk in front of the Mental Hospital while there were patients outside in the courtyard. Josie would walk a block over watching between houses to see that I was carrying out her insidious command. We would meet at the end of the sidewalk where the cornfields began and we'd walk along the secret and forbidden trail through the maze of corn until we were almost home.

It was corn season and the tall corn in the field was ripening. It was such a big field; we decided that no one would miss the few cobs we would take. Carefully peeling back the husk to check each cob we picked only the most perfectly ripe ones. When we had a good pile of ripe corn, possibly six large cobs each, we filled our shirts and started for home.

We were very proud of ourselves. We talked and laughed as we transported our heavy load. We knew that mom would be very happy and proud of us because we brought food for the family!

Uh Oh! Something seemed terribly wrong. Mom wasn't smiling. She walked out to meet us with a thin willow branch in her hand. Oh no! We'd stolen this corn after she threatened and forbade us to go into the cornfield. We thought she meant that we couldn't play in the cornfield. We picked corn for the whole family; we weren't just playing there!

Punishment was inevitable but what sort of punishment could be inflicted on children who, out of the kindness in their hearts, brought food for the whole family? Mom was a tough woman. We knew the punishment would be harsh.

When it was announced we were surprised and elated. Our punishment would be to eat every cob of that beautiful fresh corn which we had just stolen.

Josie and I decided to get started at once. First we got the fire roaring in the wood stove. We hurriedly husked several cobs of corn. They were big and golden. We got out the big aluminum pot with the wire handle and filled it with water. It was a big job for us to lift that awkward heavy pot filled with water up onto the cast iron stove. We brought two chairs near the stove, climbed up and lifted together. We were excited, chattering and drooling as the cooking process began.

Wow, this is the best punishment ever! It was hard to believe our great good fortune. We watched our corncobs dance in the pot as we waited for our corn to cook. Soon we would have our prize. Mouths watering, we cautiously lifted the big pot down from the stove, being careful not to splash ourselves with boiling water. We got plates out and heaped them high. A generous application of butter, a sprinkle of salt and pepper and we were ready for a corn-eating marathon.

Crunch, Crunch! Well, this one is not the perfect "how ripe" that it looked when we picked it and we went on to the next one. These cobs of corn were all tough and tasteless in spite of our careful choosing! Disappointed, it didn't take very long to get our fill. We wanted to stop eating and throw the rest of the cobs out but mom wouldn't allow that. She insisted that we eat every cob of stolen corn. We would have corn for every meal until it was all gone. We were most thankful that we hadn't used the wheelbarrow to transport the corn.

In the days that followed we were extremely grateful for our two-seat outhouse and the Sears and Eaton's catalogues therein. This was our punishment for disobeying, for going into the Mental Hospital maize field and stealing cow corn.

Some of our grand adventures were better than others. Today we weren't about to let a cob of tough cow corn stand in the way of our search for our next adventure.

PHYLLIS TUDOR – STUDENT DRIVER?

True, I didn't have a learner's permit but that didn't mean I didn't drive. I drove and had been driving for a long time already. Every time we went out of the town limits guess who was at the wheel? I felt powerful, talented and even mature when I was driving. I felt much smarter than most of my friends and my sisters.

My boyfriend Johnny was teaching me to drive. He said that at eighteen years old it was important to learn to drive. Johnny was nineteen and he owned a 1950 Ford, a gangster-style car. This was an old car even when I was learning to drive. Driving the car was my favorite thing to do and I was always on about getting out of town so that I could. Ya ya, some day I'd get a learner's permit but not right now, certainly not today. A learner's permit was not really necessary for me because I knew what I was doing. Like my sister Ellie, I would go straight to a driver's license.

Johnny and I lived across the alley from one another. How very convenient is that! We had been out driving but having had a late night Johnny wanted to go home and have a nap for maybe an hour. I went home too and started counting the minutes. When exactly sixty were past I went out to meet him at the car which was parked in the alley behind the garage. I sat in the car waiting not so patiently. What's taking him so long? How could he, a young man, possibly need so much sleep?

In those days people didn't always remove keys from their parked cars. Johnny was one of those trusting souls. He just knew that I would sit in the car and wait for him however long it may take. Boy oh boy, there was stuff about me that he didn't know! I had waited a long time or so it seemed. At least five minutes had passed when, hmmm! Looky what I see dangling from the ignition!

What a great opportunity had presented itself. I could practice all by myself and surprise Johnny when he came out from his nap, which I was now hoping would last a long time. That's what I'll do; I'll surprise him!

I started just backing out of the parking space and driving back in. Lookin good! I didn't hit the fence on either end or the garage. I was very cautious and drove slowly. I was proud of my skills. I became proficient backing out and driving into the parking space and this exercise was losing its excitement. Hmmm! Going up and down the alley; what a great idea! I'd drive to one end and back up to the other. This was much more challenging and it took much longer to wear thin. When it finally did, I decided that I could probably go safely around the block "undetected" by the law.

Going around the block was a great idea; however, left turns caused me concern. I went to the right which meant there was no need to cross traffic to get in or out of the alley. I hadn't really planned anything out. There was no time for planning, I was driving! Turning right meant that I would have to drive on the very busy Regent Street, the main road in Transcona. If I wanted to go on the quieter road within the community it would mean turning the car around. Ah, maybe next time through.

Slowly I pulled out of the alley and came to a stop at Regent Street. I turned on my right signal and pulled out onto the street. Approaching the next street I again turned on my right signal. Soon I was safely in the alley and in my parking space. It was so exhilarating. Maybe it was the danger, perhaps the power but I felt a need to do it again and again and again.

I decided now to drive to the end of the alley and turn the car around so I could drive on the less-busy road within the community. I signaled and turned right on the road then backed up across the alley. I shifted gears and looked up to see a police car with two officers on the other side of the street. I could have just turned into the alley and been gone. I could have just parked where I was and walked home. I could have smiled, waved or waited for them to leave. But no, that would not be me. Not enough drama.

As I saw the police, guilt completely overtook me. I was locked solidly in the grip of fear. Suddenly I didn't know a thing about driving. I was all over the road. I was all over the sidewalk. I was in gardens and between trees. The police officers were yelling for me to stop the car but I just didn't know how. Finally the car stalled and I was at a stand-still. In any other circumstance the car would have stalled before I had even moved.

I saw a family member walk past very quickly as the police officers cautiously approached. In just a moment Johnny was running down the alley to rescue me, I hoped. Who was surprised now?

Today was Sunday. I was all dressed up in my fabulous white lace suit, my stylish pointed white stilettos, my hair and makeup done to the nines. Together Johnny and I went to the police station. Of course he drove.

We were lectured by several officers at once about driving without a license. I was told to get a driving permit before I ever get behind the wheel again and to our amazement, released.

I did get my learners permit Sept. 26, 1963. The permit expired four months later, unused. Seems odd how the permit was never used. It took years to regain my confidence. I never did drive again until age twenty four years and yes, it was done with a valid learner's permit and yes, a driver's license was the end result.

A CUP OF TEE...TH

My mother had all of her teeth removed and replaced with dentures at the very early age of twenty-one years. She didn't have a specific container for her dentures nor did she have a specific place to keep them when she took them out of her mouth. As children we spent a great deal of time searching the house for those teeth, although we never ever wore them. Mother had a short memory where her teeth were concerned. She would take them out of her mouth, set them down and promptly forget where she put them. Consistently it was our fault that the teeth were missing and it was our responsibility to find them, however long it may take.

I was having a cup of milk before going to school one morning when I heard my mother getting out of bed. I quickly stashed my milk in the fridge for lunchtime and hurried out of the house so that I wouldn't have to search for the teeth. We were all sure that by lunchtime the teeth would have been found.

Mom tormented me unmercifully with those false teeth though she knew that I was afraid of them. I had frequent nightmares involving false teeth. Sometimes I'd wake up in the night and have to sing my happy song, *Rudolph the*

Red Nosed Reindeer in hopes that I could go back to sleep. I never would touch the teeth unless by accident. I could do the search and disclose the whereabouts but nothing in the world would make me voluntarily touch false teeth.

It was lunchtime and we three girls were home from school. Mom was ready to leave for work when we arrived but once again she couldn't find her dreaded teeth. We searched the house; we knew that the teeth had to be found before we could have lunch or leave for school. I was tired of looking. There were only so many logical places that they could be. We looked in each of those places one after the other, a dozen times each.

I was thirsty for the cup of milk that I stashed in the fridge earlier that morning before leaving for school. I went to the fridge to get it. As the fridge silently opened my mother who was usually quite deaf shouted to me to get out of the fridge until the teeth were found. I wanted my cup of milk and I knew that I could drink it before she could get there to stop me. At least I would have some milk before going back to school. I hurriedly raised the cup to my lips and luckily glanced into it as I tipped it up. Yuuuck! In the fridge, in the same kind of cup as my milk were my mother's teeth! She had placed the teeth into a cup to soak and had absent-mindedly put the cup into the fridge. This discovery was both good and bad. The search for the teeth was over and that was good for all of us but those dreaded teeth almost ate me alive!

POP

My younger sister and I were very close. We had spent our childhood together in adventure land and now as young adults we both lived in Winnipeg not too far apart. During our free time we continued to spend lots of time together walking miles, visiting back and forth with one another or chatting on the phone. At this time I was a bit incapacitated and confined to my home.

I was suffering a deep, very painful, boil-like pimple on my backside. It hurt me to even think about it, never mind to touch it. I was unable to actually see it, even with the help of mirrors. Sometimes I would gently rub the tender spot; it would ache and I would cry. Other times I would bear the excruciating pain and squeeze that pimple with one hand, but to no avail, it simply wasn't ready. The pressure mounted as this ugly thing grew causing it to become more inflamed and times more tender. I felt sure it would have to erupt on its own. The skin stretched over it and became increasingly tight and thin from the intense pressure.

Josie arrived at my house after one of my many teary and failed attempts. Because she is my sister I asked her to have a look at it, to which she agreed. At first she was to look only, not touch. Finally, I decided to bear the humiliation and the pain while I allowed her to press gently on the sides of it. It was so painful and I just wanted it gone. If it was looking ready she was to break the skin to relieve the pressure. I moaned and twisted under her grip. It was a torture that brought me to tears! In a tone that indicated success she said "there!" I was so pleased that the torture of this ugly thing would be over. "Did you get it?" I asked excitedly. Her answer was no. How disappointing for me!

It wasn't enough that I had this hideous deep inflamed boil-like pimple that just kept growing. I had to endure the humiliation of baring my backside as well as the torturous pain at her hand that produced no results.

CRAVINGS

At twenty-two years of age I became pregnant with my first child. I was a very nervous mother-to-be. I wanted to do everything exactly right even though the order in which I was doing things was wrong right from the start. My doctor had warned me about the dangers of excessive weight gain. At one hundred and forty five pounds, I too was concerned about weight gain. I ate very healthy and carefully. I took very long walks with my sister Josie, who was also pregnant with her first child. We walked in areas where we knew the location of every available washroom. I got a good balance of exercise and rest. I had to guess at all the changes that were taking place in my body. We were up-to-date for the late sixties but we didn't have any books to tell us what to expect when we were expecting. Perhaps we five children were adopted because my mother had no answers for any of my many questions.

I noticed that I was having occasional odd cravings that just wouldn't go away until the craving had been satisfied. The first craving was for cheddar cheese. I stalled; I made myself very busy thinking that it would just go away. The longer I stalled the more intense the craving became.

It was Sunday and all the big supermarkets were closed. I had to shop at the expensive, yet convenient corner grocery store where cheese was sold off a round. A round of cheese was about six inches thick and about fifteen inches in diameter with a thin coat of wax all around the outside. I really wanted a slice or two but my craving demanded at least two pounds. I ran all the way back home ripping off the wax and tasting the cheese with every step.

At home I started cooking at once. I cooked cheese in every conceivable way and I had a feast. Feeling stuffed and cheesed out, my strange craving persisted. I returned to the expensive little shop for more cheddar. The grocer asked what I was doing with all the cheese. I couldn't tell him the truth. I was far to embarrassed so I lied and ran all the way home.

Again I started cooking although I thought I would burst. I wasn't enjoying cheese as much as I had earlier in the day. I continued to eat until the cheese was all gone. I felt that I would be sick and I knew I had best lay down. The craving was now satisfied. I soon recuperated and decided it would be a long time before cheddar cheese would again be on the menu.

My life was going along pleasantly. I was back to eating healthy, getting plenty of exercise and rest. I felt normal for several weeks then all of a sudden whamo, out of nowhere another ridiculous craving. Now the villain was fried liver. I knew better than to stall this time.

Mom forced us to eat liver when we were children. Liver was dipped in flour and fried. Consistently it was hard, curled up, black and had the flavor of grease. I couldn't even imagine how I would be able to eat liver; yet I knew the craving would persist until satisfied. I was sure that if I satisfied the craving I would probably perish.

How is liver cooked properly? It isn't edible the way my mother prepared it! I decided to go out to a restaurant to eat. From the menu and between dry heaves I ordered liver with onions. I waited dreading the arrival of my meal. When my order arrived I was surprised that I couldn't smell grease. It didn't even look like any liver that I remembered. They must have made a mistake. I asked the waitress if this was really liver. The waitress assured me that yes, it was liver and that this restaurant made the best liver and onions in all of Edmonton.

I used the potatoes, onions and gravy as camouflage as I psyched myself up to eat liver. I had to admit that it didn't look all that bad. It didn't look as if it would have a greasy taste. Almost entirely without chewing or tasting or seeing it the liver was devoured; it actually went down easily smothered in camouflage. The craving was satisfied; the ordeal was over. I didn't die from the experience and I was only out five bucks.

I walked home thinking about how the liver hadn't killed me. I didn't even feel sick. It was nothing like the meal my mother served and called liver. I hadn't actually tasted it but I did notice how it didn't scratch my throat on the way down. My gums were not bleeding. Perhaps it was not the liver at all but the cook.

The following day the liver craving overtook me again. What a nuisance! I couldn't be eating in restaurants all the time! Why couldn't I crave something that I knew how to cook or that I liked? The craving went on for days. I made my way back to the same restaurant and placed my order again. That day when the meal arrived I ate slowly allowing myself to taste it. I examined the liver carefully to determine if it could be duplicated by a non-cook such as I. Amazingly the liver was very tasty and tender; it was moist. Yes, I believed that this could be reproduced!

On the way home I stopped at the supermarket to purchase onions and baby beef liver. The meat clerk said that baby beef was the best; I took her word for it. Late the next afternoon I felt the twinge of a liver craving coming on again but I was ready for it this time.

First the raw liver was washed then dried. Next it was dipped into an egg-wash than covered with bread crumbs. Finally the liver was fried quickly in a hot cast iron pan. It tasted so good that it was hard to believe that this was liver. I liked the way I'd made liver! Never again did I fear the liver craving, in fact sometimes liver would be on the menu even without a craving.

As an expectant mom there was a lot to learn and a lot was learned in those nine months. I had a much better idea of what to expect when expecting. If we five kids had all been adopted it didn't really matter because now I had my own experience to draw from.

MORE CRAVINGS

I found it very different carrying a baby boy as opposed to a baby girl. I found myself extremely tired all the time. I seemed to need a nap on the sofa so I could get to my bed. I had quit smoking for this pregnancy and it seemed that if I wasn't sleeping I was eating.

My first craving while carrying my boy child was for ice cream. I had to have an ice cream cone every day. It had to be chocolate, the only flavor that was also in its' very own food group. I would walk to the corner store after supper with my husband and daughter so I could get my chocolate ice cream cone. It was several blocks to the corner store, so I felt that at least I was wearing off a portion of it just in getting to it. That craving lasted a few weeks and I was very glad when it was over. The concern over excessive weight gain was great.

During this time Joey was studying for a course that would mean a job promotion for him. He often studied with one of his peers. They usually came to our apartment in Oakridge, which was within a private Jewish Cultural School, to study. At this particular time I was craving raw chocolate cake mix with raisins in it. It seemed like I ate a raw chocolate cake mix every day. I was embarrassed by this craving so I never did tell Joey about it. One day I made my cake mix with raisins but I just couldn't eat it all. There was too much left over to throw out so I decided to put it into a cake pan and bake it. The cake mix barely covered the bottom of the pan and was about the thickness of a raisin in some places.

Just as my small amount of cake mix was finished baking and the smell permeated the entire place Joey and his friend arrived. Who even knows why they were off work early that day. Both commented on how they were just in time for cake. I cringed, knowing I was busted. They roared with laughter when they saw the cake pan and they roared again when I was forced to fess up about the weird craving. I also had to make a proper cake for the two of them; they wanted it baked and iced.

As time went on during this pregnancy I found myself getting quite excited about watermelon. It was my new favorite food; how fortunate that watermelon was in season at that time. I purchased a whole watermelon every time I went shopping. In fact the need for watermelon usually determined the shopping day. I always chose the largest melon there. I was very big by this time, into my ninth month of pregnancy. Sometimes the chosen watermelon was too big for me to carry. It was the size of my belly, possibly larger. I often couldn't lift the weight. I had to ask someone else to lift it to the cart and then into the car for me.

Some of our shopping expeditions ended at home on the tailgate of our station wagon. The melon had to be cut in four pieces and partially eaten before getting into the house. That was never a problem for Tasha and me. We were happy to sit on the tailgate of the station wagon in the shade filling our faces with watermelon.

Very tired and hungry for weird cravings was a good way to describe this pregnancy. Thank goodness it was all over in nine months and replaced with a beautiful baby boy.

PART TWO

LIFE WITH CHILDREN

TERROR AT THREE DAYS

Although unmarried when I carried Tasha, I felt ready to have a child of my own. I was willing and happy to be a mother, although I didn't know exactly what that would mean. Never once did even a fleeting thought cross my mind of giving the child up for adoption. Pregnancy was going very well. It was the dreams prior to and after the birth that were difficult to handle.

No morning sickness, backache or unreasonable weight gain unlike many other women my age. There were cravings, but in general my health was very good. The greatest fear was not for my health but for that of my unborn child. My child would be born out of wedlock. I felt that I should and probably would be punished for having had a child prior to marriage, though I wasn't sure how.

Although certain the child would be a boy a name was chosen for a child of either sex. In my head a boy was desired; in my heart the desire was for a healthy baby. All the while I was tormented unmercifully in my dreams.

The dreams were always of the child and had a similar theme. The child was always a girl. She was always wearing or wrapped in pink; her hair was quite long and dark auburn. She was always abandoned, though not deliberately. I would simply forget that there even was a child. Sometimes I would be in a park with the baby; I would be distracted, walk away and forget that I had a baby. When I would remember and go back to look for her she would be gone. These dreams tormented me throughout the pregnancy.

The birth was both easy and hard. Labor lasted only twenty minutes but the speedy delivery broke my tailbone. There were about six long hard excruciating contractions. These contractions were so strong that I would pass out between them. I was given an epidural for the pain which unfortunately didn't take effect until after the birth. After the last contraction I opened my eyes. There she was, a baby girl with long auburn hair, wrapped in pink, lying in a glass bassinet beside me. I couldn't tell if this was real or if I was dreaming. She was stunning and I hoped she was real but I was horrified that I might abandon her once again if she were.

By day three I was thrilled with my baby girl. I was more than a woman who had a baby; I was an extremely protective mother! I hugged and cuddled my baby at ten pm before she was taken back to the nursery for the night. I fell into an exhausted sleep and I started dreaming immediately.

In my dream my daughter was a deaf-mute child of one-year. I had to work for a living and it was necessary to leave my beautiful child in daycare. I found the best and most convenient daycare. She always cried when I left her there. The caregiver said that it was just a momentary thing; she only cried until I was out of sight so I gave her hugs and kisses and went to work.

As a deaf mute the child had to see her doctor regularly. Picked up at the daycare, she went to the doctor for her quarterly physical examination. The doctor took a long time examining her. He kept glaring at me with a look of disgust on his face. I couldn't understand it. When he was finished he made many notes and he kept looking at me making me very nervous. The doctor told me that if he ever saw this kind of bruising on her again he would have me charged. What was he talking about? There was no bruising on her. Who would hurt a deaf mute child? Insisting on an explanation the Doctor told me that internally she was seriously bruised.

The next day I took her to the daycare as usual, there were the same hugs and kisses and the same tears at my departure. I was gone all of fifteen minutes then I returned. Through the front window of the day home I saw the trusted caregiver hurting my child. I was horrified; I was also wide-awake.

This dream stayed in my head and influenced my daycare decisions all the growing-up years of both my children. I rarely hired a sitter. I can only recall a few times that my children were in the care of someone other than myself and how unhappy they were on those occasions.

Although unwed, I was ready to be a mom. My children never caused me near the problems that my dreams did. I was grateful when at last both children were legally old enough to take care of themselves and sitters were just a bad memory.

HOW DID I GET INTO THE TV?

Tasha was always a very dramatic outgoing personality. Even as a very small child she had an insatiable need to express herself. As the first child she learned to speak very well at an early age. There were a few words that were unique to the Tudor family such as snuffle-ugg (snuggle), albalance (ambulance), mergency (emergency) and alifigater (elevator), but at eighteen months old Tasha had no problem communicating with any adult. There was, however, a problem communicating with a child of her own age. Most children her own age didn't speak as well as she did.

Because of her outgoing personality and her amazing speech, a friend convinced me that Tasha would make an outstanding little model for children's clothing. The idea was considered for a while. Was Tasha to small and to young to understand what would be required of her? At the insistence of my friend a call was placed to inquire about modeling prerequisites for toddlers.

How amazing, at that time the local Sears Department Store was looking for a toddler model for their *Spring Look 71* Fashion Show and would be thrilled to have an interview with my toddler and me. The interview went very well. The recruiters were very impressed with Tasha's ability, her petite frame and stature. They would be pleased to engage her in the upcoming show.

Soon after the interview a phone call was received. The caller indicated that Tasha's first show would be in six weeks; were we still interested and would she be up to it? Tasha was always ready to be the center of attention. Many information sessions were held during those weeks. We talked about the show, determined the clothing and accessories to be worn, the order in which they would be shown and how the models would be grouped or staggered for the most effective results. The next stage was fittings.

It was time for the first fitting. The clothing chosen for Tasha was all much to snug fitting for normal use but it gave the required effect for the stage and the camera. Dressing and undressing was tough; even Tasha was aware that the clothes were too small for her. It was difficult to get tight clothing on and off a small child quickly but Tasha co-operated like she had always worn tight-fitting clothing. With all the clothing and accessories fitting just as required for the show we were ready for the next step, rehearsal.

The first rehearsal was done in street clothes. This rehearsal was to give everyone an idea of the order of the show. The models practiced several times with an imaginary runway. Tasha was in several sets; in the first set she was with a small girl of seven or eight years old who had some experience on the runway. The next set was with a man and a woman as a family. She and the woman would be wearing mother/daughter dresses. It was obvious that Tasha was enjoying herself. She didn't need a mom; she was a fashion model. She very confidently walked down the imaginary runway and back to the exit with her different fashion show partners. She looked like she had always been a model. In a day or two there would be a dress rehearsal.

The first dress rehearsal was carried out on the same imaginary runway which was at floor level. Tasha had a very good idea of what she was doing now. She was having a good time and the show organizers were proud of her. She was the youngest model in the show and she was enjoying all the attention coming her way. The next dress rehearsal would be the day of the show at the Bayshore Inn, in downtown Vancouver. How would Tasha do on a narrow runway four feet off the ground? This would be the first time for her to walk on the actual runway. Come rehearsal time she was amazing. She strutted right out to the end of the runway as though it was still level with the floor.

The rehearsal was being video-taped and there was a monitor backstage. Those people backstage could watch the show and stay on time for their sets. Tasha had done supremely well for a very small child. She noticed the monitor as she came off the stage and thought she was watching television. She enjoyed seeing familiar people on the monitor. In a few short hours the actual live evening show would be underway.

There were lots of bright lights and a loud hum could be heard as the audience filled the large room. One of the ladies involved in the show asked Tasha to look for her in the front row at the end of the runway. As Tasha and her partner walked out they would be reminded to look for her. When Tasha stepped out on stage and saw five hundred strange faces looking at her she was surprised and she shrunk back a bit. None of the many rehearsals had prepared her for this part of it. Her young partner sensed her fear. She smiled at Tasha, tugged gently on her hand and they started off down the runway. She was visibly relieved to hear the familiar voice of daddy in the audience. She was also happy to see the familiar lady waving at her from the front row. The girls waved as they did their spins and then returned to the exit in perfect time. The show was going very well and the children were a huge hit. In a few minutes the long-awaited show would conclude. We could relive it again and again in our minds or we could watch it on television in two weeks.

On the night the show aired the family gathered in the living room. Our black and white television set was turned on and we waited for the *Spring Look 71* Fashion Show to begin. As the show commenced Tasha recognized many people. She was very excited when she saw herself on the television. Suddenly she realized that she was watching television in our living room and she was on television at the same time. How did I get in the TV mommy? was her most urgent question.

THE SPAGHETTI TREE

Ryan was about eleven months old. Although his hair was quite long, it was naturally curly and the curls stuck to his head like pin curls. His hair was so fair as to be invisible on his head. Ryan was the cutest little fellow around. He was the youngest member of the family. Then there was Sparky his big dog who was older by six months.

Ryan and Sparky were inseparable buddies; they shared everything. They napped curled up together on the floor. They shared puppy cookies, toys and they always shared Ryan's meal.

Spaghetti was Ryan's very most favorite meal in the whole world. He loved long spaghetti with homemade sauce. I never did know if it was the taste, the texture or the fun he had eating it that made it his favorite meal. He seemed to like the feel of the slippery noodles in his hands. He liked to slurp up those long noodles one at a time. There was always a surprise when the noodles would whip around and slap his little face. Sometimes the noodles would stick to his arms, his chest, his hair or his high chair. Spaghetti was a very messy meal and he usually ate it wearing only a diaper, as he was transformed into "The Spaghetti Tree."

When Ryan was finished his meal I would remove his dishes and tray. It was certain that the next step for him would be the bathtub. While I was busy cleaning up after my baby, Sparky would busy himself cleaning his bestest buddy. Ryan giggled aloud as Sparky's tongue would tickle his whole body one lick at a time. Ryan would then escape from his highchair and run to the waiting bathtub, while Sparky would find a cache of spaghetti that had previously been hidden or out of reach.

Ryan was satisfied. He ate his favorite supper, shared with his bestest buddy and was happily playing in the bathtub. Sparky was satisfied to get a taste of people food. He cleaned up his bestest buddy, cleaned up the chair and he was ready for a nap. In spite of the mess the day always ended well as the spaghetti tree blossomed, bore fruit, was harvested and then went into dormancy waiting for the next season.

TEX

Alan was fifteen when he first made his home with the Brandow's. It was strange having a fifteen-year old along with a four and two-year old. He was much older than my little babies but not to old to be in school.

Alan was enrolled during the school term at Burnsview High School, in grade ten. He knew that going to school was a condition of staying with us. It isn't easy to fit in as the new family member and as the new high school student at the same time. Al tried. He kept up with his chores at home and he got involved in school rugby.

Rugby is a very rough sport and it was hard for me to support Alan in it. While attending his games, most often my head was turned or my eyes were closed. When Alan was not in his rugby jersey he was usually sporting his familiar western shirt, jeans, and the shared brown cowboy hat.

Alan loved to dress western. We had many horses and ponies and western dress was appropriate for him. We only had one good cowboy hat which was shared by the family. After a while the house rule was, *the first person up in the morning with the hat on his head had the privilege of wearing it for the day.* We all wanted that hat and morning became a scramble. At school Alan was teased about his manner of dress. In a derogatory way some called him Cowboy; others called him Hotdog or Tex. He wasn't pleased about it but he didn't make a fuss either. He was too busy riding his horse in his spare time to worry about foolish and possibly jealous classmates.

Alan bought Dusty, his horse, with his own money. Dusty was a pure white gelding of no particular breeding, of whom Al was very proud. He spent every spare moment in the saddle riding miles on Dusty along with Joey, a more experienced rider on Zeppelin, a more spirited horse. Sometimes on their excursions the rest of the family was allowed to trail along, Tasha riding Choo Choo, Ryan doubled with his daddy and me astride Fury pulling up the rear. Alan had not even touched a real horse prior to living with us but he mastered horseback riding quite quickly.

Dusty did anything for Alan. He would rear up and walk on his hind feet; he would walk sideways or backwards, he would also kneel and bow. Dusty always knew who was in control. Whatever they may say at school, Alan was mighty proud of his finely-honed riding skills.

It was nearing the end of the school term and most classmates were willing to accept Alan for the western personality he was. A field trip was being planned for year-end. The class was thrilled to be going horseback riding at a local dude ranch for an afternoon. The riding skills ranged from one end of the spectrum to the other.

At the ranch the students were suited up with mounts matching their various skills. Most of the horses were tired overused nags that could think no further than returning to the barn to eat hay and to rest. Those riders who claimed experience were mounted on some more spirited animals.

Two of the classmates who claimed experience were Doug and his twin brother, the class bullies. Alan modestly claimed experience and the three were mounted on some very headstrong, with an attitude-type horses. Alan was at ease with his horse. He had ridden Zeppelin often enough and was familiar with the proper methods of handling the lively spirited animal. The twins were not having such a good time.

Doug and his brother spent a good deal of time walking in circles as their skills became apparent. When the guides were ready to lead off everyone kicked their mount to get them going. Some students had to kick for every step their horse would take. The horses plodded along the trail in single file as they were accustomed on a trail ride.

Alan and the evil twins were to bring up the rear. They would be responsible for keeping all the horses on the trail. Al was clearly up to the challenge. Slowly the large group moved out. It was a casual ride through pasture, woods and meadow. There was plenty of opportunity to commune with nature and relax. The twins, however, did not relax; in fact they were having increasing difficulty with their spirited mounts.

The twins were unable to keep their horses on the trail; they were galloping here and there in circles. Alan was keeping a close eye on them. It was clear now who was master. Suddenly the horses bolted and got their heads. The distressed, soon to be thoroughly humiliated riders latched on to the saddle horns for dear life.

The saddle horn is commonly used to mount or dismount the horse, in securing the stock when wrangling or the place to carry the lasso during round-up. To ride holding the saddle horn was the defined mark of an inexperienced rider. Although he was probably snickering under his breath, Alan resisted his urge to gloat as he leaped into action.

Galloping as fast as his horse could move, he raced after the runaways. He pulled up between the two. Using his knees to guide his horse he took their reins in hand. They were led back to the barn where the evil twins, no longer oozing evil, willingly dismounted to await the return of their classmates and a hefty helping of humble pie. They were grateful for Alan's expertise, their rescue and for having their feet safely back on solid ground.

Alan rode away in haste to re-join the trail ride. There was a new respect for him in the group. Everyone had seen the incident with the twins. Perhaps Al had saved their lives! Was he in fact a hero? On the bus ride back to school the twins were understandably quiet.

Everyone was exhausted from the busy afternoon of riding. Some complained of sore legs and backs, while others yawned and stretched out in their seats, some even napping during the ride home. They were all sweaty and dirty from the trail.

The bus ride conversation centered on Alan, his skills, his courage, his presence of mind and the amazing rescue. Alan lay back in his seat, feet stretched out into the aisle. His arms folded across his chest, a single stem of grass hanging from between his faintly smiling lips, the brown cowboy hat pulled down shading his baby blues; Alan was relaxed and quietly enjoying his new found notoriety.

At the age of fifteen our Alan fit in nicely as a new family member, a new high school student and an awesome class hero. Some peers still called him Tex and other names but they smiled now and said it with a new respect for him.

THE EMPERORS NEW CLOTHES

Tasha was five years old when she was modeling in the annual Sears *Spring Look 75* Fashion Show. The show was held at the Newton Inn in Surrey, home territory. Backstage was the hallway; it was also an entrance into the motel. The models had to cross the hallway to change clothes and to go back out on stage.

Tasha and another small girl were going out on stage together with Winnie the Pooh. They had to be helped up to the runway. Tasha and her partner would walk Winnie the Pooh to the end of the runway and back as the narrator gave her commentary. Tasha had a very quick change before her next set. We had a rehearsal earlier that day and found it would be best if she were changed backstage rather than the dressing room so she would be dressed, coifed and ready in time for the next set.

The show went on as scheduled. The little girls were on stage with Winnie the Pooh. Waiting backstage for Tasha, I held everything required for the quick change. As I waited I glanced toward the motel entrance at the far end of the long hallway. Walking towards me were three young men who all looked amazingly alike. Looking from the darkness into the light of the doorway it was hard to see more than silhouettes.

These young men all had big hair. They were all the same height. They all sported a scruffy beard and moustache. As the three approached me I wondered if they were triplets! These young men smiled and spoke to me as they walked past. My eyes were not yet adjusted to the light. It was a surprise to see them go out on the runway. They weren't a part of the show, according to my recollection or program. The crowd was laughing and gasping and suddenly everyone knew that they were not a part of the *Spring Look Fashion Show*.

On the other side of the wall the crowd calmed. The little girls came off the runway dragging Winnie the Pooh. Tasha let go of Winnie's hand and came stomping over to our pre-arranged meeting place. She was utterly disgusted as she demanded to know how come those boys didn't have any clothes on.

Amazing! Backstage in the hallway waiting for Tasha three young men walked ninety feet toward me, they smiled, they spoke to me and then they walked out onto the stage. They certainly looked alike. That fact is not surprising as they were also all dressed alike, in their birthday suits. These young men were three of the many streakers of the 70's. They had come to model *The Emperors New Clothes* at the Sears *Spring Look 75* Fashion Show.

CASUAL CONVERSATION

The adults sat in the dining room chatting after breakfast while two year old Ryan and four year old Tasha watched *Sesame Street* in the living room nearby.

The conversation was light and silly though the topic was serious. We were talking about when we die. Alan declared that he wanted to be buried at sea; Joey wanted to be buried in the ground. If my only choices were fish or worms then I wouldn't be able to decide right now. Tasha, who was listening to us while she watched the Sesame Street program, came into the dining room to announce that when she dies she wants to be very old.

The topic then shifted and now we were talking about what to wear to the up-coming wedding. Joey complained that he had no clothing suitable for the occasion and he may have to attend Don's wedding wearing nothing but his birthday suit. Tasha didn't know what a birthday suit was and so she questioned her daddy. Daddy told her that your birthday suit is what you were wearing when you were born. The small child looked at him and laughed as she informed him, "Daddy, that won't fit you anymore, you're too big."

A block of commercials interrupted the Sesame Street show. Tasha was listening to the commercials when she heard one that she just knew would be of benefit to her little brother. The commercial was for one-a-day vitamins for people who don't eat right. Tasha came running excitedly to tell what she had heard. "One-a-day vitamins mommy, for people who don't eat right; we should get some one-a-day vitamins for Ryan cause he doesn't eat right, he eats with his hands."

WHO'S THE MOM?

A nine-acre hobby farm in Surrey, BC was home when the children were young. It's a wonderful experience for children to grow up in the country. We raised chickens, ducks, pigs, calves, ponies and horses. Some animals were for food, some were for pets, some for recreation and others for work. Tasha and Ryan still wanted a pet bunny each to complete our menagerie and finally they wore me down and I gave in to their hearts desire.

At the Langley livestock auction we looked at all the bunnies prior to the sale and chose those that we would bid on. The auctioneer started to sell rabbits. It was positively thrilling. This would be my first time ever to raise my hand and bid at an auction sale.

Ah, the bunnies that we chose! Quickly I raised my hand again and again, possibly even bidding against myself in my excitement. The auctioneer hollered SOLD and banged his gavel down on the block. We were entirely unaware and somewhat annoyed to learn that bunnies are not sold individually but in litters. Now we were the anxious new owners of seven young bunnies. Five more bunnies than we wanted.

We managed to sell one bunny as we took these new family members out the door of the auction. We asked the same price that we had just paid. When we arrived home a friend bought one each for her three girls. Only three bunnies remained and we were clearly relieved. We could live with one extra bunny.

It wasn't long until a lot of commotion could be heard coming from the barn where we decided to make a home for the new little bunnies. It seemed that the children wanted all the animals to meet and they were busily introducing them. Sparky, our big dog, was also invited in to meet the new arrivals. He was thrilled. Sparky thought that the children wanted to feed him lunch so he took his choice of the bunnies and he left. The hysterical children were devastated by this action. Now we had the number of bunnies we originally wanted, "two."

These two bunnies were content to live in our cozy barn. They were given a full bale of hay in which miles of tunnels were built. This is where they played and scurried to hide from the curious children. They seemed very happy in their new home.

A former neighbor had a pet bunny that she kept in a cage at her home. Sadly the family suffered allergies and the bunny needed a new home. Barbie would give up the bunny willingly if it could come live with our bunnies so that it would have friends. We agreed to take care of the bunny and it was put in the barn with the other two. They all seemed to get along well.

Soon after, Daddy and Alan were in downtown Vancouver shopping when they spotted a lovely silver/gray bunny running loose on the very dangerous Granville Street. The instant decision was to capture the bunny and take it home where it would be safe from the busy traffic. The capture was a success and now there were four bunnies growing up at our farm.

It seemed no time at all until those babies were all grown up. After school each day Tasha took Ryan out to the barn to visit with them. This particular day they both came crying to the house to inform me that the bunnies were fighting. There were clumps of hair everywhere in the hay. We all rushed back out to the barn to see what the commotion was about. Well, after a phone call to the Vet, it turns out that the bunnies were not fighting at all; they were having young. Pulling chest hair out and into a pile was the way they built a nest in preparation for their newborns.

The hair clumps were white and all the bunnies had white chest hair. So who, who was having babies? We would have to find the mom somehow and put an end to this straight away. These bunnies would have to be separated. We tried but could not determine who was what sex and we still didn't know who the mom was. Another pile of white hair! Oh no! This means more newborns.

Things started happening very fast now. If only we knew who the mom was we could get them separated. The babies were getting quite mature by now. They must be separated today. It is very difficult to determine the sex of a rabbit at any age, although the males didn't seem to have that problem. These bunnies were separated every way that we could think of by size, by color, by age, but by now the babies were having babies. The days of being anxious and worried about seven little bunnies were fresh in our minds and we longed for that time back. Raising bunnies at our farm was completely out of control. If we were trying to raise rabbits for food this would never have happened. We would have had sterile rabbits.

When there were about a hundred bunnies and that happened rather quickly, we packed them all into cages and returned to the Langley livestock auction, this time as vendors. We kept only the original two rabbits, in separate wire cages.

THE FARMER MILKS THE COW

We lived on a nine-acre hobby farm in Surrey, British Columbia. Ryan and Tasha were young and we had sixteen-year-old Alan, our foster-son, living with us. It was fun living in the country. On our hobby farm we kept chickens, pigs, calves, bunnies and ducks. We had many horses for our riding pleasure and ponies for pony rides; the rest of the animals were just for fun, for pets or food.

All the people in the neighborhood lived on small acreages. One neighbor had a lovely Jersey cow that demanded milking at the same time every morning and evening. It seemed like a lot of work to have a Jersey cow. Going on holiday was hard for these neighbors, bordering on impossible. They were tied to their farm by a Jersey cow.

An opportunity arose for these neighbors to go on a fishing trip and they desperately needed a holiday. They begged throughout the neighborhood for someone to take on the cow-milking duties for four days. Joey had a week off work so after much begging he volunteered to milk the cow morning and evening for the next four days. He had grown up on a farm in Saskatchewan and he had experience milking cows. It was settled then and the neighbor left before Joey could change his mind. Within minutes of the neighbor's departure the telephone rang. It was Joey's boss asking him to work. He would have to drive a load to Edmonton that same night. "So who would milk the cow now?" I wondered.

How much does one need to know to milk a cow? It was hard enough to find a volunteer in the neighborhood now we had to find one in our own family. Oh thank goodness! Alan said that he knew how to milk and he volunteered. How grateful I felt knowing that it wouldn't fall on me.

As it approached cow-milking time the young volunteer wandered over to the heavy-laden cow that was patiently waiting in her corral. Alan was away about an hour when the family began to be concerned about him. We had no idea how long it took to milk a cow. Perhaps he was kicked or somehow hurt by the cow. Hand in hand we three crossed the pasture and climbed over the fence to see how he was doing. When we arrived there wasn't a single drop of milk in the bucket or anywhere else. Alan now confessed that he had no idea whatsoever of how to milk the cow but he was sure that it would be easy. My entire cow milking experience came from watching television. Milking a cow was not my heart's desire and watching the cow milking process on TV was far less than perfect training. It did not provide enough knowledge to actually milk a cow by hand. My greatest fear was being realized. The cow milking duties were falling on me.

Cow milking should be similar to all nursing mothers. Hold the teat gently from the top between thumb and pointer finger, push up to stimulate than squeeze gently and pull down. Yea, that's it! Milk! It wasn't like a hose but I was getting milk. It was a relief for me to be able to relieve that cow. She was probably in agony because it was now so late and it was taking so much longer than what she was accustomed to. Although my hands were slow and clumsy she made no fuss as she began to feel some relief. After about five minutes of milking, there were minimal results in the bucket; a clear indication that it was going to take a very long time to complete this task. I wondered how old I'd be when my pail was full. My hands were not familiar with this type of work and were feeling sore. When at last the milking was complete my arms and hands were unable to lift the milk pail to move it from under the cow. Never before had these hands felt such pain. Alan returned to retrieve the ever so precious milk, to feed the cow and to set her free in the barnyard.

By morning my hands were no longer numb but still quite sore. The cow was waiting for me at the barn door. She watched me arrive with my sore hands and empty bucket. Wow, this is hard work! It's much harder and it is taking a lot longer than I ever expected. My wrists were now as sore as my hands. When my work was done Alan and the children had to go over to retrieve the bucket of milk once again. They fed poor old Bessie and set her free in the barnyard. My hands ached the entire day and now, darn, it was time to milk the cow again. Would these four days ever pass? There were still two long hard days left. Four more laborious milking sessions then I was done. Joey was going to owe me so big time for doing this to me, for letting me suffer like this.

After the third day my hands and wrists seemed less sore. Perhaps muscle was being built up. At any rate cow milking was going well now. Bessie may not have been getting stripped as well as she was accustomed but that cow was getting used to me. She was grateful to be milked at all, even by these inexperienced hands.

We had such an abundance of milk by now that it was impossible to use it all; yet the thought of giving any of it away was seriously resented after having worked so hard and suffered so much pain to get it. Milk and cream were on the menu every meal these days. Our fridge was overflowing with dairy products and there was still one more day of milking. Alan was busily preparing supper, which became his job when I took over milking. He was pouring the cream off the top of the milk when, to my dismay, the gallon jar "slipped" from his damp hands and one whole milking session splashed to the floor and ran into every crevice. I wanted to cry and stomp and just be angry but at this moment I was far too busy cleaning up glass and milk.

Today was the last day to be the reluctant cow-milking farmer. This new experience couldn't be over soon enough. Never wanting to see a cow again, my heart knew that poor old Bessie was waiting at the barn door for me completely unaware that I hated her with every fiber of my being. I do have to admit though, that it was taking less time each session and she was being stripped better each time. Gratefully the morning session was completed. The balance of the day was spent hoping that the neighbor would get home early enough to relieve me for the evening session. But no, my life is not like that and poor unfortunate Bessie had to contend with me one more time. At long last it was over. I fed her for the final time and set her free in the barnyard. With my well-earned pail of milk on my arm I crossed the road, climbed over the fence and hustled across the pasture to the great home base. Such a nightmare it had been, yet amazingly we had all survived it.

The telephone rang. On the telephone was the neighbor home from his relaxing yet profitable fishing trip; he was calling to thank Joey for milking the cow in his absence. A truck rolled into our driveway; it was Joey returning from his "escape" trip from Surrey to Edmonton. I'm so relieved that the torture is over; I'm sore from the intense and foreign type of work and I'm angry with Joey that I ever had to do it in the first place.

I felt sorry for these neighbors; they were tied to their farm by a Jersey cow. Future holidays for these people was beyond bordering on impossible if it were dependant on me or anyone else in my family, it was completely out of the question. Within days of their return the Jersey cow was being bred, no longer requiring that regular am/pm milking. I couldn't help wondering why they didn't breed Bessie before they went on vacation; it would have saved everyone, especially me, a great deal of grief.

I AM A RO-DE-O RIDER!

Alan was looking forward to participating in the local Langley rodeo. He had a special custom bareback rigging built for his event. Alan usually rode only in the bareback competition. This year he felt he needed a new challenge and he entered the calf-roping competition as well, not knowing what that might mean in terms of preparation.

It takes a great deal of time and patience to learn to use a lasso well. Alan purchased a lasso and began to diligently practice every day. He learned to swing that rope over his head, in front of him and any other way that was humanly possible. Being fast and accurate is essential to win the calf-roping competition and he was determined to win. Now this young rodeo rider practiced every spare moment every single day and he may have even slept with his rope in his hand. It was like the rope had become an extension of his arm, it was always in his hands and he automatically roped everything he came near. He roped posts, bikes, stumps and anything that moved. What Al really needed were some fast moving targets. Our calves were fed up. They didn't even bother to run from him anymore, they would just lie down in the pasture.

We boarded several horses on our little nine acre farm, including three ponies belonging to my friend's children.

Dee would pick up her girls after school. She would visit and play cards with me while our girls aged five to twelve went out riding their ponies for an hour or so. They rode in a large pasture that was free of trees where they could get going quite fast. From inside the house we could hear them shouting and laughing. We knew they were having great fun racing and showing off to one another.

When Dee was ready to leave we went outside together. We watched the children for a while then had them unsaddle, brush and walk their ponies before turning them out. To our surprise they were all tearing around the pasture with Alan in hot pursuit, his lasso swinging over his head closing in on the young riders. The lagging rider appeared to automatically become the next target. Alan would throw the rope, tie it to the saddle horn, stop and the rider would hit the ground. The young riders enduring Alan's unique practice techniques suffered many scrapes and bruises at his hand.

Alan never did get fast enough that year to ride in the calf-roping competition. He attributes his unfortunate lack of success to the whining, crying and poor sportsmanship of his fast-moving targets.

THE LANGLEY RODEO

Although Al had been riding horses for two years, he had never even touched a live horse until he came to share our home. He loved to ride and he would do anything that would get him outdoors and onto a horse. His dream and his long-term goal was to go on a long trail ride through the mountains, his short-term goal was to ride horseback anywhere and anytime an opportunity presented itself.

The Langley rodeo was coming up. Alan and Joey talked about the possibility of horseback riding from our home in Surrey to the Langley rodeo grounds for the event. Mostly they talked about the fun they would have along the way and the adventure of not knowing exactly where they were going. They charted their route by road. However they would not travel by road but on horseback through fields, ditches, pastures and woods all divided by barbed wire fences with very few gates. Little thought was given to preparation or the possible challenges they could and probably would encounter en-route. Many trips were made to the location as they mapped out the general route they would take. The purpose of the map was so I would be able to find them easily.

Plans for the trip were crystallizing now the route, supplies, departure and arrival times. The date was drawing near. Alan decided to challenge his skills further as he now registered for the bareback and saddle bronc competitions. At the very last second and to my absolute horror Al also registered for bull-riding.

All those plans were now firm, tomorrow morning they ride. Up at the break of day the men prepared a lunch and a drink for the trail. It was my job to meet them along the way to provide snacks and water for them and water and feed for their horses. They saddled up, mounted their horses and headed out early that Friday morning to begin their long adventure ride to the Langley Rodeo Grounds.

The cool of the morning burned off by about ten o'clock and became scorching heat by mid-day. Thank goodness for woods and shade. The trail wasn't quite as simple as it had been in the car or in their planning stage conversations. They hadn't accounted for bridges, fences without gates and honking cars that caused the horses some anxiety. Their estimation of time was also off considerably. The hot afternoon cooled as evening approached. As the moon and stars lit up the clear sky about eleven pm Al and Joey hungry and weary arrived at the campground.

The tent was already set up and a small fire was burning in the pit. The men brushed and watered their horses then tethered them for the night; they were exhausted and so were the men. A few minutes of bragging around the campfire and it was off to bed for the two of them. Today had been a big day but tomorrow would be the main event.

They arose at ten o'clock in the morning and got the coffee perking while they tended to the horses. Breakfast consisted of hot dogs and coffee on an open fire. There was a buzz of excitement in the camp as the contestants prepared their rigging. Some polished boots while others shone up buckles and spurs. Still others rosined up their gloves or practiced for their event. As morning became afternoon anticipation mounted and an enthusiastic rodeo crowd started gathering.

The festivities were to commence at one o'clock within the chain link fenced area and they would continue until eight o'clock in the evening. Al was excited; he got dressed in his new jeans, his gray suede chaps and the new red cowboy shirt made especially for this occasion. The shirt was red in case there was blood. Firmly planted on his head sat the very cool shared brown cowboy hat. The finishing touches were a red bandana tied around his neck and shiny new jangling spurs.

The Grande Entry parade would open the festivities. Alan, along with many fellow contestants, would carry a flag in the parade. How proud he was astride his pure white gelding with the pink eyes and nose and with his flag blowing in the breeze. Later Al pranced around the grounds showing off his new western duds talking to everyone he met. He wanted to ensure that people recognized him when it was his turn to ride.

His first event was bareback riding. The horse was prepared with Al's custom-built bareback rigging. During that preparation time Al applied a last minute coat of rosin to his glove. The high-spirited horse was getting very excited. As Al lowered himself down onto the horse's back the rigging was cinched tightly around the girth. The horse fell in the chute and a re-ride was called. The second time the chute opened and the horse bucked his way around the enclosure for five or six seconds before ridding himself of his rider. Al hit the ground and jumped up running almost in a single movement. His hat remained firmly on his head.

His next event was saddle bronc riding. An association saddle (a saddle without a horn) is used for this event. The cinch was pulled tight as Al lowered himself down into the saddle. The chute opened and the horse bucked wildly. Al spurred and raked for the full eight seconds before he was tossed aside. The whole family stood at the fence jumping and cheering. It looked like a great ride to me worth at least a hundred points but no points were awarded by the judges once again.

Al's last ride and the last event of the day, bull-riding! He just had to try it. Imagine concentrating long enough to spur and rake while sitting on the back of a huge angry Brahma bull holding on with only one hand. Well, that is the scenario one would expect to see but Alan's bull sauntered out of the chute and proceeded to calmly walk in circles. The bull didn't buck at all and a re-ride was called. The second ride was wild and very short, much less than the required eight seconds. Again in a single motion he hit the ground and bounced up running as the rodeo clowns leaped into action distracting the mount.

The closing ceremony marked an end to a marvelous day of excitement and adventure at the Langley Rodeo. No prizes were awarded for his efforts today, only the fun he had and the experience gained. Already tired from the long ride there, a short sleep on the hard ground, a full day of being tossed around by big nasty rodeo stock Alan now had to prepare for the long ride home in the dark.

Alan and Joey started their ride to the great home base soon after the closing ceremony. They were both on an excitement induced high. They bragged and boasted about their talents all the way home; Joey bragged of the good old days while Alan bragged of today. They would arrive home in much less time than it took to reach the rodeo grounds. In the wee small hours of the morning stiff, sore and tired they dismounted and tethered their horses in the back yard. Although their bodies could barely make it to bed, their spirits soared.

Al learned to ride as a teenager. He continued to challenge himself until he was ready for a rodeo. He learned the value of solid plans and diligent preparation also how the trip is much faster and incident free in the planning stage. He lived his heart's desire to go on a long ride and to ride in a rodeo. The thrill of the rodeo was now in his blood. His love of horses has never waned. The entire adventure has caused his spirit to soar and it has taken him to a whole new level of horseback riding excitement.

NOW THE SUN SHINES!

On our nine acres in Surrey we kept several ponies. When my niece visited from Manitoba, we went to the horse auction in Mission to buy a pony for her to ride during the summer. She named her little pinto Petite because she was a Shetland pony. Petite was more than just a pony; Petite was a mother. She had a fuzzy little white foal that we named Muffet. She was very small and young; she stayed close to her mother at all times.

It had been raining hard for a week or so as it often does on the lower mainland. The pasture was deep in water and even the ponies were tired of the rain. When the last drop of rain fell and the sky looked like it might clear, the ponies came out from their shelter to find a bite of fresh grass to eat. Poor ponies, they had to walk through deep water to get anywhere in the pasture. They were feeling frisky after being confined for so long, anxious to stretch their legs.

Baby Muffet began to stretch her little legs, near her mother at first then she ventured further and further away. She didn't seem to mind the water at all. We all laughed at her because she was so cute. This was her first time to stray more than ten feet from her mommy. She knew that she was the star of the show now so she hammed it up running as fast as she could. Each time that she came near the fence she looked up at us to see if we were still watching. All the other horses and ponies stood by watching her too.

Muffet ran far out into the pasture. She pranced around out there with her little tail arched high in the air, looking very majestic. She began to gallop back to her mom when, UH OH! Poor little Muffet! She fell in the water face first and slid on her side for about twenty feet. We were all afraid that she would be hurt. She came to a stop and looked up at us. Muffet got to her feet, shook herself off and trotted into the lean-to out of our view.

The clouds dissipate; now the sun shines. And little Miss Muffet; well she is humiliated and hiding in the lean-to behind the barn alone, by herself, with nobody.

ONE PEAR

On the farm in Surrey there were many fruit trees. Each person in the family had his own cherry and apple tree. There were a large variety of apple trees. There were many cherry trees, several plum trees and one single pear tree. We were told that each fruit tree requires a mate tree for cross-pollination. The yard and the small pasture were beautiful and wonderfully fragrant in the spring when everything was in bloom and in fall when the fruit ripened the branches were bowed by the weight of the fruit. This made for happy horses, cows, chickens and children who spent a lot of time under these trees.

Tasha and Ryan kept an eye on the pear tree. It had been covered in blossoms in the spring but they couldn't see even one pear growing on the tree. They checked the tree every day. Those children pretty much lived in the trees when the fruit was ripe. They would climb off their ponies onto the lower branches than climb high up into the trees where they would stay until they ate their fill.

One afternoon they were riding slowly around the pasture checking out the fruit trees when they discovered a pear. One single pear hung all alone high up in the tree. They were ecstatic and they trotted over to tell mommy of the discovery.

They tried several methods to get the pear down but it wasn't ready to fall. Each day they rode their ponies out to further investigate the status of the pear and each day they tried another ingenious method to bring that pear to the ground. I glanced out the window where I saw both children in the corner of the small pasture beneath the tall pear tree. They had a bright red hula-hoop which they were tossing up into the tree in an effort to fell that lonely pear. They made many a failed attempt chasing the hula-hoop all over the pasture.

I could hear the children cheering. They must have been successful in bringing the pear down. They ran excitedly to pick up that precious pear from the ground but when they got there they didn't pick it up! It was the prize; why didn't they pick it up? They stood looking down at it for a long time. Distressed, they came to the house crying. "Mommy we got the pear down but it fell into the fresh cow poop and now we can't even have it!" they reported.

All fruit trees need a mate tree for cross-pollination. How odd that we had the only pear tree in the neighborhood and that only one of those millions of spring blossoms was pollinated resulting in a harvest of one pear!

BARBED WIRE

As a three year old, Ryan was often rejected or neglected by his sister and all the older daycare children. When they went riding on their ponies, Ryan was left out because he needed a parent with him to ride. When they went on adventure hikes, Ryan was not fast enough to keep up. He was also too short to see over the long grass or to see what might be hidden in that long grass. He was just too small to do a lot of things that older bigger kids could and did do.

It was tough being the youngest child. Sometimes Ryan would excitedly start off with the others kids. He would soon lag behind and when they would not wait for him or they would disappear out of his sight, in tears he would make his way back to the great home base and mommy.

Today daddy was planning a hike to the woods to mark some standing dead trees. We had a wood burning fireplace and it was a great adventure to go out as a family to find, cut down and haul the wood home. A hike out to the woods would be necessary to first locate and mark the trees. With flagging tape in his pocket and an anxious group of small children at his heels, daddy was ready to set out.

All the children were ready to go on the hike including Ryan. They were all dressed in long pants and shoes; they also wore hats and long sleeves to protect them against sharp branches, ticks and anything else they might encounter. As a group they started off for the woods. Everyone was chattering excitedly. I watched until they were over the hill and out of my line of sight. Some time later I wondered how they were doing and glanced out the kitchen window. There in the pasture was little Ryan making his way back to the house. He looked so sad and dejected slowly though loudly stumbling across the pasture.

I slipped on a light jacket and shoes then went out to console my young son. I called his name as we both approached the barbed wire fence from opposite sides. Ryan was closer to the fence than I. He ducked under the wire but he didn't move ahead before standing up. The barbed wire captured him by the back of his jacket. As he walked away the wire dragged him back and hung him on the fence like laundry. Unable to touch the ground with his hands or his feet he was indignant about the capture. He cried out of anger as he awaited mommy's arrival and certain rescue.

THE GARDEN OF EATEN

We lived in Surrey on a small acreage. It was the ideal place to raise a family, some winter food and to grow a lovely garden.

We had ponies for pony rides, horses for our riding pleasure, bunnies and ducks for pets, pigs for winter meat and chickens for eggs and meat. There were lots of out-buildings to accommodate all our country critters. There was a barn for the pigs, one for the chickens and the ducks, although the chickens were free-range during the day. The rabbits had their own shed filled with hay and the horses and ponies had a barn and a lean-to for shelter. There was even a small pond for the ducks.

The property was divided into four pastures. The pasture nearest the house was filled with fruit trees and it was the smallest one of the four. The entrance to all out-buildings could be accessed from this pasture.

I wanted a vegetable garden but the yard was too small to accommodate it. I was sure that the soil in the small pasture was fertile enough to grow a lovely garden. I proceeded to move the fence in that small pasture so that all the out-buildings could be accessed from the yard. Now there was plenty of space for a vegetable garden.

With great care I dug and tilled until the garden area was ready for planting. Everything was planted in neat even rows. Because of how they grow, I planted Hubbard squash on a little hill at the foot of the garden and pumpkins on another little hill near the barn.

Everything grew quickly and beautifully in that wonderful Lower Mainland weather. Soon we were eating fresh vegetables from our garden. Hubbard squash and pumpkins are very much autumn vegetables. I could see them growing just beautifully. Huge dark green squash and beautifully-shaped pumpkins rambled over the two individual little hills.

It isn't easy to keep the dreaded free-range chickens out of the garden but I did a good job of it. These chickens started to run as soon as they saw me coming out of the house and the garden continued to be chicken-free.

Early in the fall I had a close look at the squash. They sure were looking good. I walked out to the little hill they were growing on just to lift one up to find out how heavy they were getting. Imagine my surprise when I lifted one of these huge specimens, almost falling backward down the hill. The squash that should have been very heavy at this time each grew into empty shells.

Every giant squash on the hill had a single hole in it near the bottom. Each hole was about three inches in diameter. It was just the right size for a chicken to put its head through as it devoured the entire content of the squash. Only the dark green shell was left. These huge squash continued to grow in spite of the hole to the hefty weight of a few ounces each.

The acreage in Surrey was a lovely place to raise a family, some winter food and to grow a garden. Who knew that my wonderful vegetable garden would become a self-serve diner for my winter meat!

TRAVEL

Travel with children is not easy even before luggage is considered. My family was traveling from Calgary to Winnipeg on the train when the children were only four and six years old. We packed as light as possible for the trip but we still had a large suitcase and a canvas shoulder bag.

When traveling on the train only the coach is assigned. Coach seats are on a first come first serve basis. When the train starts loading there is a lot of loud noise, a frantic rush to get out on the platform and a race for the assigned car to ensure seats together. It was like a herd of cattle that day stampeding down the platform. I was afraid for my children. I was unable to hold their hands because I had to carry the luggage. I had the kids hold on to my jacket pockets one child on each side of me.

I could feel them holding on to me but I couldn't actually see them. Sometime along the way I looked down to make sure that they were still both with me. Tasha was there on the right but I couldn't see Ryan. The bag on my shoulder was pulling on my jacket and it felt like Ryan was holding on but he wasn't there. Where was my baby? I dropped the luggage and we started back in tears shouting his name and pushing through the oncoming crowd. We informed the conductors of the situation and they assisted with the search.

When we got back near the beginning of the platform we saw a small frightened child. It was our little Ryan alone, afraid and crying. It was painful to see my baby is such distress. I picked him up and hugged him tight so grateful for his rescue while a conductor hustled us back to our coach.

A travel decision was made that day. Never again would we travel anywhere without holding hands. When we reached Winnipeg and arrived at the bus terminal to continue our journey we had a one hour wait. We put our luggage into a locker while we went out shopping for backpacks for each one of us.

When we returned to the locker containing our luggage we opened our huge heavy suitcase and started to transfer all of our belongings to a large backpack for myself and smaller ones for the children. Anything that didn't fit into the backpacks, couldn't be carried or worn went with the suitcases into the garbage.

Travel with children is never easy. We traveled often and we learned how to pack amazingly light. From that frightful day forward we traveled with backpacks so we could hold hands to keep track of one another.

FINGERTIPS

We drove to Okotoks from Calgary to visit Ralph and Joey, our former neighbors. Okotoks was a very small town and seemed far out in the country in 1976. We had supper and a great visit there with our friends. When the children aged five and seven started getting restless we went on a hike to help wear off some of their excess energy. There were wonderful hiking trails and lots of fun adventures for the children along the way.

Eventually our hike brought us to the Sheep River. We walked west along the river until we arrived at the Sheep River Park. There were lots of campers and fun-seekers walking and playing in the water that early spring day. The water was low, its temperature tolerable. We removed our shoes and socks to our backpacks and waded into the water. Quickly we felt comfortable in the chilly water. There were many small islands due to the low water. We walked on the islands looking for special stones, shells, sticks or any treasure that we might find there. Some parts of the river were slow narrow streams while other areas were swift. We avoided those swift areas; we knew the danger.

Ryan, my friend Joey and I were busy collecting treasures when I sensed that Tasha was in trouble. Just as it occurred to me, I heard her frantic scream for help and my hair stood straight on end. I left Ryan with Joey and I began running for Tasha. She seemed so close yet I was unable to reach her. She slipped on some rocks and fell into the water in which she was playing. This innocent looking water was too fast moving for her to regain her upright stance and now she was floating past me on her belly, feet first.

Tasha was floating away as fast as I could run without shoes. I hadn't noticed all the broken glass, sharp rocks and short bushes before. Now all those things were preventing me from reaching my little girlie pie. She was screaming franticly and her eyes disclosed her terror. Tasha was getting too far ahead of me. Her little arms reached out for the mommy she knew and trusted to save her from this brutal river. How could the sun dare shine so beautifully on a day when I could lose my only daughter? I was moving far too slowly. I couldn't let her get any further away.

I was unable to run on the rocks in bare feet; I was already cut and sore. There was no time to stop and put my shoes on; anyway they were in my backpack on the shore way back there. I knew that the only way to catch up to and rescue Tasha was to get into the water. I lay in the chilling water, which for me was not deep enough to swim. The cold water helped me forget about my own cut feet. Kicking hard I started to half swim, half float very fast toward Tasha, who continued to float very fast away from me. There were many large pieces of driftwood and rocks impeding my forward motion. We were whipped around curves, over rocks, around small islands and bushes all the time getting closer but still out of reach. The water seemed to be a wider, deeper stream now but the current was just as swift. I was grateful for the deeper water and the greater momentum I was achieving. We were almost touching now, fingertips apart. We could see into one another's eyes. It was painful to see my precious daughter that I loved so dearly appear so frightened while I struggled to reach her. We talked all the time. I tried to reassure her that Mommy would rescue her, while she continued to cry and scream in fear. In my head I planned her funeral and tried to imagine life without her.

I kicked my feet more franticly in an effort to move up that half inch allowing our fingers to touch. At last we were touching and soon I had a solid grip on her. We were both crying now. I held her tight as I turned myself to use my feet as a brake against the rocks. We sat at the water's edge for some time holding one another and thanking God for saving our lives. I carried Tasha out of the water and we rested on the small island for a while. We were grateful to get out of that river when we did because just beyond this point the river became a wide and raging torrent which may have devoured both of us.

We had to catch our breath now in preparation for the long barefoot journey back to Ryan and Joey. It would take us a while to get there. We had to walk the entire distance over the rocks and things which we had previously considered treasures. We had to do it now with bare feet and exhaustion.

In our efforts to wear off some excess energy we discovered how important and life-saving a generous reserve of excess energy can be.

RYAN BRANDOW– RESPONSIBLE DRIVER

As the kids were growing up I always allowed them to shift gears in the car as I drove them to school. My car had a standard transmission and they felt very grown-up knowing when to shift gears by listening to the motor. Ryan was first to want a driver's license and he was willing to do whatever it took to get it.

I taught him how to shift gears according to speed and engine sound so that he could drive a standard transmission. I had a friend who owned a private airstrip with a proper gravel road, which is where Ryan learned to drive. So I wouldn't teach him any of my bad habits, I let him drive alone on that private road. He could use only first and second gear while he was driving alone. All power poles were to be considered stop signs for the purpose of practice. I would entertain myself with some target practice while he drove.

When he was doing well, I sent him to driving school to learn all the other facets of driving. At last the big day came. He was ready to take the test. He was both excited and nervous. Ryan knew that he knew what he knew but would the tester see his confidence?

He had practiced every day and was able to shift gears very smoothly without a hint of jerking. He checked his rear-view mirror regularly. Ryan signaled and shoulder-checked with every lane change or turn he made. He drove the speed limit or less. He kept the proper distance between himself and the vehicle ahead. He was as ready as he could be. The test would be completed in my car.

The test came and went. All that anticipation, the raw nerves and Ryan said the test wasn't even hard. He passed with flying colors and held his certificate as proof in his hand. His smile of satisfaction went from ear to ear. He had set a goal for himself and he attained it. I was very proud of my young son. At last he could drive without his Mom. He could drive with his friends, if he could con his mom out of her car.

The very first licensed evening Ryan asked if he could take the car. The condition for using the car was that he had to drive me to work and pick me up afterwards. He dropped me off at the CGH with instructions to be on time to pick me up. He drove away and I went to work. I was confident in his skills but concerned about other drivers he would meet on the road.

About an hour into my shift I noticed that the sky was black in every direction; it would rain very soon, possibly hail. I hoped that Ryan would be safe at home when the rain started. When the rain did begin, it was torrential. In minutes the CGH parking lots were flooded. Many cars were sitting in water that was above the bottom of their doors. Traffic was very slow due to the street flooding.

It was a very stressful shift. Most of my time was spent looking out the window and trying to phone my young son, whom I was unable to contact. On the job I watched the news; there was major flooding throughout Calgary and lots of damage to homes and vehicles.

By nine thirty pm the sky was clear and blue; it was hard to believe that we'd just had such a wicked storm. People were now pushing cars out of the parking lot and assessing the damage. One hour later I finally got in touch with my young son. Ryan and his friends had gone home when the rain started. They watched out the window as the street flooded and put many drivers into distress. Ryan, with friends Cliff and Ian, spent the rest of the evening helping people get their cars to higher ground. Some cars were pushed uphill to the sidewalks, others onto the meridian or the lawn. They worked very hard all evening; all the time my car was safely parked in its' own parking place.

I was very proud of my son for taking responsibility and keeping off the road during this horrendous rainstorm. I was also very proud of him and his friends for having the courtesy to help people in distress without extorting money from them.

Ryan was the first licensed driver of my children. He had to make a lot of important decisions on his first day as a licensed driver and he did very well. Parking the car was probably the best decision he made that day.

SCAREDY CAT DOGS

I traveled to Merritt, BC to visit family that lived just outside of Merritt in Lower Nicola. The kids usually waited for me on the hill along the highway when they knew that I was on the way. It was always fun to visit and take them on an adventure walk. Our adventures always included a mixture of exhilaration, danger, excitement and a little touch of the forbidden.

It was a dreary overcast day when we took our three dogs Max, Sandy and Houston on a long walk. No plan, just a walk. We walked through every graveyard we came to. The graveyards were all native, as Lower Nicola is a predominately native community. We read the names and dates on the grave markers as we walked through. It seemed that a huge number of these graves were of young people. The kids always pointed out the graves of people they had known and told the stories of how they lost their lives. As we passed through the last cemetery we decided to hike up to the gravel pit.

The path to the gravel pit was all uphill; it was also all sand. We walked for a long while on this twisted path allowing the puppies to run freely, sniffing, barking and marking today's territory. To pass time we sang songs, chattered and laughed aloud. When we finally reached the gravel pit we realized how far we were from the road. It had been a long strenuous hike and we were pooped. We needed a rest so we found a place to sit down.

The rest ended as a rather freakish feeling about this desolate location and our being here at this late hour of the day crept up on me. It felt like the perfect place for a murder and the hair on my goose bumps stood on end. Without discussing my feelings about the place, we started heading back to the road. We traveled quickly sometimes sliding in the sand, sometimes running down the hill making our way back to the road. Our progress downhill was much faster than uphill, even considering the many times we had to stop to empty the sand from our shoes. After a few stops and a need for speed, it became a competition as to who could walk with the most sand in their shoes, who could jump the farthest into the sand below and who could empty their shoes the fastest. We could hear the traffic below and knew that we were getting close to the road. A few more leaps down the hill and we were grateful to be on level ground and on the path leading to the road.

It was getting dark now. Our dogs were put on short leads because we would have to walk on the road all the way home. There was a deep ditch filled with water and not much of a shoulder to walk on, along this busy two lane highway. We had to walk in single file most of the distance.

About two blocks from home lived two ferocious German Shepard dogs. They always did a lot of barking and curling up their lips, snarling at all passers by. Today with their teeth bared, they looked like they might cross the road to eat us all alive. We had never seen them as bold as today when they chose to come out to the centre line of the highway. It was awkward walking with three children clutching onto me in fright.

We were feeling nervous huddled together. Even our little dogs were nervous as we tried to hustle past this heavy danger zone. Suddenly and all together, the three scaredy cat dogs leaped into our arms completely reversing the protection order.

It was always fun to visit the kids and take them on an adventure walk. Our adventures always included a mixture of exhilaration, danger, excitement and a little touch of the forbidden. We all looked forward to these visits knowing what they would mean, yet never really knowing what they might include.

HARE HAIR

It was one of those special nights when my children wanted to sleep in my bed with me. Their usual con line was, tell us about the olden days, please mommy. Of course it worked tonight as it always did. They tuckled (snuggled) with me and we talked about the olden days until they fell asleep. I enjoyed having them tuckle with me so when sleep overtook me I didn't disturb them. I dozed off with one child on each arm, briefly recalling, yet willing to accept the consequence of such an action.

Near morning something woke me. It wasn't a noise necessarily; it was more a feeling. Someone was in the bedroom aside from us and our dog hadn't barked. It was at that moment I realized my arms were asleep, numb from fingertip to shoulder. I was filled with terror. I couldn't move to protect my children or myself. I lay there horrified by my thoughts. Now I could feel movement at my feet. Oh my goodness! What's going on?

I could do nothing about the situation so I didn't move nor did I open my eyes. I didn't want to see what it was that would surely kill all of us. I was glad that the children were both asleep and would never know what had happened. What was the point of being more afraid than I was right now or worse, frightening my innocent little children? The movement and pressure continued up my body inch by inch and was now on my chest. I knew that whoever it was would soon go for my throat. Still there was only numbness in my arms.

I could feel something touch my chin and lips. It felt prickly and made me want to sneeze. "Whiskers," I thought! With numb arms I still couldn't protect myself! The waiting was too much for me; I just had to see what was there before it killed all of us. I opened my eyes. Almost too close to see was Buggsy our adorable litter and house trained rabbit; her long whiskers poking into my skin. I gasped when I saw her. I was ever so relieved to see that it was Buggsy but I didn't want her to take another step and hop on to my face.

An amazing chain of events followed. As I gasped, the sound frightened her. The bunny turned and leaped away onto Ryan's head. Ryan woke up frightened and shouting which scared the bunny and woke Tasha. The bunny jumped off the bed onto the sleeping dog that jumped up barking loudly. All the commotion woke the neighbor's dog in the other half of the duplex. That dog barked and woke the kids next door who started banging on the wall. By now we were all wide awake and laughing hysterically at the bizarre sequence of events.

I loved to have my children sleep in my bed. I didn't encourage them but I never refused them either. I loved telling them stories about the olden days while they tuckled on my arms. Having numb arms from fingertip to shoulder was a small price to pay for having the pleasure of their company throughout the night.

SMALL WORLD

Daddy promised to take his children to Disneyland. How they looked forward to that trip. They talked about it all the time with their friends. But then, daddy was gone. Could this be the end of the dream? How could his children ever get to Disneyland now?

It was not easy being a single parent. I was working two jobs to save for the coveted trip to Disneyland. Every pay period saw those savings grow a little bit more. By late 1983 the saving was complete and I came home to meet the children with a great many dollars in my hand. Excited didn't start to describe them. They looked at all that cash and knew that they would not only take a trip to Disneyland but they would have plenty of spending money while there.

We talked about when we would like to go and unanimously decided to be there at Christmas. We had never been away from home on Christmas Day before, but we were prepared to make the sacrifice. Immediately we phoned to book our holiday and rushed out to pay for it. Disneyland was guaranteed now and was the only conversation in our home for the next two months. Such model children could never be found anywhere else.

December the 23, 1983 finally arrived and we were to board the plane at four thirty pm. At about two in the afternoon we received news that our flight would be delayed. We kept checking in, another hour and another two. When at last we boarded the plane ready to leave it was eleven thirty pm and the aircraft was buzzing with the sounds of excited but seriously over-tired children. With the late start and short night the children barely slept at all. In fear that they could still be prevented from entering Disneyland, they were up at the break of day begging mom to get up so they could enter the world of adventure.

As we arrived at the ticket window to purchase our passports, we felt a thrill of excitement. We passed through the gates, looked in awe at our surroundings and realized that it would take a long time to see and do everything before us. It was hard to decide what to do first. There were rides with long line-ups, shows popping up out of the ground, parades, characters walking around, souvenir shops and a wide array of food vendors.

On Christmas Day we decided to spend the entire day in the park and have our dinner there also. We arrived as the park opened and the line-ups were short, however it wasn't long until the park population tripled and quadrupled along with the line-ups. By dinner time we were feeling mighty exhausted. We went to the nearest food vendor and made our choices hoping to be recharged, so we could stay longer. A short distance away, we found a large round table with seating for fifteen. We sat down people-watching and quietly eating.

As we relaxed at our table a band came out of the ground singing and playing. We commented on how we were in just the right place at just the right time. There was nothing to obstruct our view and we were enjoying the show. As we watched, some kids came to sit at the front of our table. We didn't mind their presence. It was a big table and they were small.

The show concluded and sunk back into the ground. We were finished our dinner by now and had been revived, ready for another walk around the park. The kids across the table turned around and looked up at us. What a surprise it was and what a small world we discovered we lived in when these kids all looked at one another knowingly. They were not just kids from Calgary but from our own neighborhood and to make the world even smaller, they were friends from our own school.

MONSTER RABBIT AT THE HORROR SHOW

There was a birthday party taking place at our home that night. There were lots of kid's tuckled (snuggled) together on the comfy grey couch. They were all sharing one big blanket. Some kids were screaming, others hiding their faces in the blanket while others were bravely eating popcorn. They had insisted the doors be locked, the curtains closed and the lights be turned off for this frightening movie.

These brave kids wanted me to watch the show with them. I am not a fan of scary movies. I can scare myself just fine thanks. I didn't need a scary movie for that. I declined their request and made my way to the basement. Sometimes I could hear them squeal or gasp as they tried to be brave.

After a while the telephone rang. They shouted for me and I hustled up the stairs to answer it so they wouldn't be interrupted. I left the basement door open and the light turned on in my rush to get the phone. I sat in the semi dark kitchen chatting quietly with my friend. The only light in the room came from that open basement door which shone onto the back door.

Suddenly I could hear the kids screaming. I peeked into the living room to see what was happening. To my surprise the kids were not looking at the television; they were all looking at the back door. I felt a chill and my hair stood on end as I turned to look. There on the back door and to my relief was the six foot tall and growing shadow of our little bunny. She had followed me up the stairs to star as the monster rabbit at the horror show.

DAM BUILDERS

Larry was working with the forestry that summer. He was located at the Ghost Ranger Station near Cochrane, Alberta where he was flying initial attack. He invited us to come out to the station to camp for the weekend.

It was the long weekend in July when we packed for camping and drove out to the ranger station. The road was gravel and very winding as it followed the creek. It seemed that lots of campers were in a hurry to get to the campgrounds as they were speeding past on that already dangerous and narrow road. We were pleased when we finally arrived; happy to be off that race track. We were excited about camping, especially about being in a private campground. It was a campground reserved for fire-fighters in the event of a dangerous fire requiring a great many fire fighters.

The station was vacant; no one was around. They were all out flying on an initial attack mission. Only the cook was available. We chatted with him for a while. He told us that the guys wouldn't be back for some time but he could give us directions to the campground if we wanted. We walked over to the fence together. The cook pointed as he said, "You can go through this gate and across this field. See where the trees are parted over there? Go through there. You will have to go down the hill for a ways and you'll have to cross the creek five times in all. Don't worry though, the creek is very low right now. After you have crossed the creek four times you'll see a fork in the road. The good road goes up and the bad road goes down, take the bad one. You'll cross the creek one more time and come into an open field by the beaver dam. Keep going to the stand of trees on the left and you can set up camp there by the river. I'll let Larry know that you have arrived."

We started off through the field questioning our sanity. Those directions sounded pretty off-the-wall. Ok, so we were into the forest! The hill was steep. The creek was lined with rocks and only a trickle of water, we crossed it easily. The so called road was only wide enough to drive; there would be no turning around, no matter what we encountered. At last, a possible place to turn around. This must be the bad road he was talking about. Oh good, we only have to cross the creek one more time. Finally we were in a field and there's the beaver dam! We made it and it wasn't all that bad. We crossed the field and arrived at the stand of trees where we parked the car in the shade. Everyone got out of the car now to look for the perfect place to set up our two tents close together.

The place screamed adventure. We got our tents up and a fire started in a hurry so we could pursue one. Ryan took out his pellet gun while Tasha went for a swim. We were right at home in this place at once.

After a while we could hear the sound of a helicopter approaching. Larry was coming to look for us. We stood out in the open waving and shouting to him. Like he would hear us!

That first evening we went walking up the hill to meet Larry. It was light when we started up the path. What fun it was walking back in the woods in the night and by the light of the moon, a little bit of stumbling but we all had a great time.

We cooked our first supper over the perfectly burned-down fire and played capture with the kids as supper cooked. We had ropes and tied the kids up, sometimes to trees. They had a great time trying to escape, which they did every time. As we ate, Larry told us a beaver dam story from his youth. He explained how he and his brother had caused the dam to leak by pulling out some sticks and how the beavers came to repair it. We chuckled but we didn't believe it. It was just one of the many stories he told us.

We had a fabulous time on our own the next day. There was a new adventure wherever we went. We took a hike up the creek, swimming in every deep hole we found. We found a place to target practice. We spent time around the beaver dam hoping to see a beaver close up but there were none to be seen. Again in the evening, we walked up the hill along the creek path to meet Larry then we'd walk back down together in the dark.

Tonight, as we prepared to go up the hill we stopped by the beaver dam. We wondered if that story he told was true and we knew that there was only one way to find out. We all started to take sticks out of the dam. Everything was woven together. They were amazing builders. It was not an easy job to remove anything from the dam but we finally did manage to and a few subtle leaks were started. We washed our hands in the creek and carried on up the hill. On the way back we would know if the story was true.

As we started back toward camp we told Larry about our mischief. He was pleased and he said we'd be amazed. The full moon and stars were bright in the country sky, almost like daylight. As we neared the bottom of the hill Larry asked us to be quiet so we wouldn't disturb the beavers. We walked quietly and when we arrived at the dam we all sat in the long grass on the bank.

There were beaver! We watched in awe and in silence as some beaver brought sticks. Some stayed at the leak building while others brought mud, stones, moss and any other building supplies they might need. It seemed like they had to take things apart in order to weave it all back together solidly. It was most amazing to watch the well-coordinated team efforts of those industrious little creatures.

Suddenly the old grandfather beaver rose from his lookout point. This is the place from which he oversaw the entire build. He scurried quickly down the hill. He slapped his wide tail on the surface of the water to issue a warning to the family. He dove into the dark water. He too, had been sitting in the tall grass. He sat between Tasha and Ryan who were frightened by his movement and scampered up the hill to grab my hand. As grandfather beaver slapped his tail on the water issuing his warning he dove to the bottom out of our sight; all the other beaver snapped to attention. Soon the show was over as all the industrious construction workers followed grandfather deep down into the dark water and out of our view.

In the morning there was nothing to indicate there had ever been a leak in the structure. The dam was completely repaired like new and not a single beaver in sight.

LEAP OF FAITH

I was in the upper level of our house glancing out the window into the back alley. I could hear Ryan and his friend shouting back and forth from a distance. I knew that there was construction in the alley so I was looking out to check on their safety.

It seemed that the construction in the alley was not a hindrance to the boys of the neighborhood. It may have even been just the challenge they were looking for. Barriers were to stop cars, not boys on skateboards or bikes. Boys attempt dangerous feats just to see if they can. Just to say did you see that or look what I can do!

When boys were competing on bikes nothing is unusual. It was not uncommon to see feet in the air above the fence as the boys rode by doing a handstand; holding on to the seat and the handlebars. Nothing is unusual or out of the ordinary with them. As I glanced out the window to see what the boys were shouting about, I spotted Ryan on his skateboard shouting to his friend Luke far down the alley and quickly approaching a construction barrier. As I tried to open the window to shout a warning, I saw Ryan leap the barrier only to land back on his board on the other side of it, still shouting and still riding. It was like the awesome move was planned in advance, which he might like me to believe. I, however, think that it was one of those, opportunity presents itself, did you see me kind of a tricks, a leap of faith.

SUR-PRI-SE

I met Casey at School when I went back to upgrade my education. Although she was much older than I, we became great friends. She had problems in Mathematics, in which I did well and I had problems in English, in which she excelled. It was a great match and we helped one another, mostly on the telephone.

Casey had decided to move from her high-rise apartment where she lived on the seventeenth floor, to a basement suite in a three storey building a short distance away. I had a car so I often brought it full of packing boxes for her. The plan was that she and I would move all the boxes in my car and her daughter and son-in-law would bring the furniture in his truck.

The day came and we started moving the boxes so that there would be only furniture left in the old apartment. As we moved the boxes, we put them into the appropriate rooms at the new apartment. The boxes would be out of the way at both ends and it would be easy for her kids to move and place the furniture. The move went well and was complete by early afternoon.

The only glitch was that the four seat sofa would not fit into her apartment. Not straight on, not without legs and not on end. It was simply too long. Casey was very concerned. She couldn't go out to purchase another one, nor could she be without one. She was a poor university student. It was a huge dilemma to which she could see no way out. Her son-in-law Rupert said that he would come back to take it away if need be.

We decided to move the sofa up against the wall in the hallway while we organized her new apartment and thought about the problem. It was a small apartment and it didn't take long to organize. We were all tired. The kids were hungry and it was time to call it quits. The caretaker said that the sofa would be fine where it was for a few days. I told Casey not to worry, we'd come by tomorrow with my tool box, my sewing machine and a bunch of garbage bags. We said good night and went home.

In the morning we arrived as planned. Casey had been unpacking and she was showing me some fuzzy brown fabric that she found. Suddenly we had a plan. I asked Casey if she cared what size her sofa was. She didn't understand what I was saying but she said that she wished it were a love seat. At that we decided it would be better if she stayed in the apartment and I stayed in the hallway and the kids became our runners.

I started to uncover the end of the sofa. As I took pieces apart I sent them with the kids to Casey who was to use them as a pattern for that brown pile fabric she found. As we worked one pleasing step led to the next. It wasn't long until what used to be the old four-seat sofa was the skeleton of the new love seat. We stopped for nothing. The kids made us coffee and lunch. We kept working as we ate and sipped coffee, neither knowing what the other was doing but believing that it would all work out.

By evening we finally came together to see what was happening and how we were doing. Sur-pri-se! We were both astonished by our handiwork. There sitting against the wall in place of a four-seat sofa was a beautiful newly-covered love seat and several green bags of old fabric, stuffing, springs and wood. We took the green bags to the garbage and brought the new love seat into the apartment.

We were both thrilled with our efforts. The love seat fit well in the room. When Pat and Rupert asked about the sofa they didn't believe what we had done. When they actually saw the love seat they asked where she got it. Casey had faith in my expertise as a carpenter and I had faith in hers as a sewer. Her only concern was what would we do with the garbage bags and now she knew.

TORNADO WINDS

It was the summer of 1986, a beautiful sunny day of an unusual weekend, unusual in that today I was not working. I spent the morning biking with my dog following hot air balloons, of which there are many in the weekend skies of Calgary.

Tasha and her friend had a small birthday party catering job this afternoon in Bowness. They were so excited about doing this job on their own. So grown up, they were older teenagers who felt sure that they could handle the job on their own. I would drive them over and pick them up in the evening when the job was done. They would call me so I wouldn't be waiting around or more likely so that I wouldn't be giving them any direction.

That afternoon as we drove to the community of Bowness the wind was quite strong as we passed the Deerfoot Trail going west. We all commented on the wind and how it was affecting driving. Although it was rather warm outdoors we drove with our windows shut. As we drove away from Memorial Drive the wind seemed to calm down some. We drove through the community until we reached the Bowness Recreation Centre. I went in with the girls to find out what was required of them. Feeling confident that they were capable, I said good-bye and went home.

The girls called me three hours later. They were in the process of final clean-up. If I were to leave at once they would be done at my arrival. I left home straight away. The wind seemed to be getting strong again. It's odd how the wind in Calgary seemed to be only on Memorial Drive west of Deerfoot Trail, as though that area of Memorial Drive were a wind tunnel. Once again as I made my way into the community of Bowness, the wind calmed down. I arrived at the community centre just in time to help the girls finish up. They had a marvelous day as catering ladies and they were well-paid to do their work.

When the last dish was put away, the counter and floor were clean, we walked away. It was evening now. We drove casually toward home since there was no rush to get there. We were back on Memorial Drive when we started noticing broken tree branches on the ground. There were branches on the road, most were small but some were quite large. The further we went on Memorial the more branches there were. It was like being in the Twilight Zone because we were the only car on the road; at least we were the only car we could see on the road with all those branches. Soon we had to turn off because the branches were too big and too deep to continue. We left Memorial Drive and traveled on Sixteenth Avenue returning to Memorial near the Zoo. There were still branches on the road, however, they were smaller and fewer. It was as though a Tornado had gone through Calgary, only on Memorial Drive.

We continued to have strong winds from the west. Edmonton also was having strong winds. There were tornado warnings for Alberta. Who even thinks of tornadoes in Alberta? It wasn't common. The following week, on the radio, we heard that in Edmonton a tornado had touched down wreaking havoc in a mobile home park. It destroyed many homes leaving the families homeless. Twenty-seven people died and the damage totaled three hundred thirty million dollars. Debris, including furniture and appliances, was scattered for miles around.

Calgary weather is not very predictable even from one neighborhood to another let alone day to day. In one community of Calgary there were hot air balloons floating by; at the same time in another community of the same city there were tornado winds.

KANANASKIS STYLE SKI POLES

After the age of forty I learned to ski, both down-hill and cross-country. I loved the idea of screaming down hill fast, yet remaining in control. I liked that the same trip could be taken at a more leisurely pace, allowing time to enjoy the view and the experience. I also liked the idea of being on the level, swooshing along the groomed trails, enjoying all the magnificent winter countryside. The calm and quiet of the woods was alluring. I already owned down-hill equipment, now at last I outfitted myself with cross-country ski equipment and I headed out to Kananaskis Country to break them in.

I loved the fresh air and the quiet of the mountains. Now and then I would hear a Whisky Jack or a Stellar Jay cheeking me off for intruding on their space as I swooshed along the trail. Houston, my Sheltie, would usually cheek them back with a loud bark and break the wonderful silence. The crackling of the fire on my return warmed my heart, along with my cold hands and feet. The aroma of the hot chocolate and the toasted marshmallows reminded me of how much I loved the great outdoors in God's country! I would go there as often as I could.

Skiing is a very exhilarating sport. I just love to be out in the snow either screaming down the hill or gliding casually through the woods. I have never been able to determine which sport I prefer. Each is the ultimate form of winter sport when I'm participating.

Houston would always come with me to cross-country ski. On this particular occasion my daughter Tasha and my friend Mae accompanied us. Packed for a wiener roast and dressed in layers, we loaded the car.

We had a favorite ski location that we would frequent in the wide open spaces of Kananaskis Country. The trail at Evan Thomas was five miles long, filled with curves and hills and beautifully groomed. There was a fire pit near a picnic table when a rest was required. We were all in need of a good stretch when we reached the location. Houston leaped out of the car. He ran around marking the area that he would claim for the day; Houston knew where he was. We started a fire in the pit and unloaded the car onto the table. Mae filled the water kettle with snow and put it on the fire so that the wait for hot chocolate on our return would be short.

The morning air was crisp. It wasn't long until we were on our skis and ready to go. Mae was going to walk on the ski trail with Houston and maybe take a picture or two while Tasha and I skied. We made our way to the trail and were about to take off when we realized that something was missing, something very important! How could we walk away from the car without our ski poles? We'd have to go back to get them. When we arrived at the car we discovered that they were not there either. We forgot to bring our poles? How could we forget our ski poles? We came to ski, we wanted to ski and we would surely ski before we went home.

I am the person who is always prepared. I would've made a great Boy Scout if I hadn't been a girl. I carried fire starter, Swede saw, matches, paper, blankets, extra mitts, scarves, boots and hats. I carried a shovel, an axe, a knife and a walking stick. I carried whatever I thought I would need for wherever I'd be. I was ready for most situations and I would find a solution to this situation also.

We took our skis off and started to look at the small trees around us. We were looking for trees that were tall enough without being too thick in the trunk making them heavy. It didn't take long until we had four perfect poles made and we were ready to ski away. We let nothing stand in the way of our plan.

The day warmed up considerably and we made the most of it. We would ski five miles then return to the fire pit for hot chocolate, a marshmallow or two and to strip off some of our clothing layers.

We had a delightful day. We skied to our hearts' content. Our ski pole invention worked marvelously; our wiener roast was perfect. We all got the fresh air and exercise we craved. The sun was going down; we were exhausted and it was time for us to leave our favorite ski trail.

When we arrived at home, we found our factory built ski poles pushed deep into the snow, inside the yard. We'll have to break them in next time out.

WHO'S AFRAID OF THE BIG BAD WOLF?

It was about 1985 when Larry gave me a Browning lever action twenty two caliber rifle with a scope. I had always been afraid of guns up to this time and he decided that I needed to learn to use one for life in the country. We found a great place for target practice and I became a crackerjack shot. Soon I was training on bigger guns with more power and kick. Occasionally we went to the Kananaskis Gun Club for target practice where we arrived looking like Mr. and Mrs. Rambo with all our guns slung over our shoulders and hanging off our arms.

When Larry felt I was up to the challenge he offered to take me deer hunting. We read through all the hunting regulations and looked over all the area maps. We decided on an area that was not too far away from the great home base. It was a place that we could drive to early in the morning and drive home from at dark.

On a Sunday afternoon prior to hunting season, we went to scope out the area. Parking off the road we climbed through the barbed wire fence and entered the woods. We were on an animal trail immediately. It felt wonderful to walk in the woods on a cool fall afternoon. It was a thickly-treed area yet without leaves on those deciduous trees it felt open. We walked a long time before we were unable to see the road. Good place to be as I felt the urge of nature calling out for relief.

In my life it is only at the most inopportune times that nature would call. Luckily it isn't hard to find a potty in the woods. They're everywhere! Behind every tree, behind every stump, behind every bush an open-air potty awaits. I found a suitable one without any difficulty. Larry walked slowly ahead and kept talking to me as I quickly removed my many layers of clothing and carried on with my most urgent business. The air was crisp and some exposed areas of my body were feeling chilled. With my business out of the way I reapplied the layers and hurried along the trail to catch up with my fearless leader.

From arms-length behind him I began to reach for his shoulder. As I raised my arm a huge wolf in his magnificent winter coat leaped between us. He passed through looking directly into my eyes not touching either of us and then he was out of sight. It was eerie to have direct eye contact with a wolf out in the wilds. Larry didn't even see the creature; by the time he turned around the wolf was long gone.

There would be no more potty breaks and no more walking in the woods for me today. I wasn't feeling much like Mrs. Rambo as I ran as fast as I could to the safety of the car. Years later in my mind's eye, I can still see that luxurious winter coat and those curious gray eyes as they looked into mine.

I wanted to go hunting. I had trained with all those guns and was an amazing shot. I simply didn't expect to meet anything wild in the woods. Perhaps I just didn't understand the real meaning of the word hunting. So, who's afraid of the big bad wolf? Well, I guess it's me!

Part Three

There Is Life After Children!

KILLER MOSQUITOES

When we made the decision to move from Calgary, AB to One Hundred and Fifty Mile House in central BC, I was educated about the location with many stories. It was heavily emphasized that the mosquitoes were plentiful and very, very big. I know that there are many types of mosquitoes in varying sizes, but I wondered if this story might be a bit exaggerated. Having never been to the location, I was at the mercy of the storyteller and accepted the stories as truth.

It was the end of June when we arrived at One Hundred and Fifty Mile House, Stampede weekend in Williams Lake thirty minutes away. On our second day there at the ranch Larry flew back to Edmonton for a few days where he had an appointment and Ryan took the bus back to Calgary so that he could spend some time with his friends there. I was alone, by myself, with nobody on our quarter-section of land located in the middle of a two-thousand acre agricultural lease. The mosquitoes were in full force when we arrived. I found them to be plentiful and irritating but certainly nothing I couldn't handle. I carried my bottle of mosquito repellant in my pocket at all times and applied it liberally as needed. It wasn't long until I smelled like

Muskol and the uncovered areas of my body were a mass of raw, oozing mosquito bites. I looked like I had met with a terrible plague.

There I was on the back balcony surveying my new surroundings when nearby I heard a loud and suspicious zzzzzzzzzzz. Uh oh, my heart leaped to my throat. What is that? It must be the sound of one of those giant mosquitoes I'd heard so much about. I couldn't see it but I did hear it and I knew that it was nearby eyeing me up. I headed for the back door at once when I heard it again. It even sounded big. zzzzzzzzzzzzzzz. Oh my! It was right in front of my face. It was so close to my nose that I had to look cross-eyed to see it at all. The story was confirmed. It was a gigantic mosquito just as the story told! The killer stinger was at least two inches long and the mosquito moved like lightning! My life began flashing before my eyes; this mosquito would certainly kill me! As quickly as it arrived it was gone. Not hungry I guessed! I hustled indoors closing the door behind me to escape the beast.

My heart was pounding. I was breathless. How could I get to my car to make my getaway? Larry had been right about these mosquitoes; but why didn't he tell me more about them? What kind of repellent would be effective against such a creature? The sting of just one was sure to cause death. Thank goodness that my children were not here. I sat at my kitchen table for a long while trembling! I didn't want to look out and see these creatures that would surely be the cause of my demise! How did people carry on jobs; what about children and animals? Nothing would be safe from these mosquitoes!

I was going to be forced to look out the window. I had to plan a defense against them. I watched for a long time but saw nothing; yet I knew that they were out there watching and waiting for me. Every now and then through the locked window I could hear one out there in the distance, zzzzzzzzzzzzz it called to me.

I stood at the window for some time and now with my nose pressed hard against the glass. "Where are they?" I wondered. "Why can't I see them?" They are as elusive as any other mosquitoes! What is that which I see on my clothesline? Oh my! Is that one of those killer mosquitoes? It must be! It looks like a small bird but it does have a two-inch stinger which gives it away. Could that be a bird? If that's a bird, it's the smallest one I've ever seen!

I dug through many unpacked moving boxes in search of my newly-acquired bird book. I wanted to look for it, knowing all the while that I wouldn't find anything like it. Wow! There it is! It's a ruby-throated hummingbird with a two inch beak. It summers in South and Central British Columbia.

TO WATCH YOUR CHILDREN GROW UP

Tasha was always a very independent child. She would watch what I did and then she would copy me. At every stage of her childhood she enjoyed doing anything that allowed her to feel more grown-up than she was.

When I would collect the laundry it could usually be assumed that any clothing on the floor in the children's rooms was in need of laundering. I thought after a long while that I was washing the same clothes for Tasha week after week, yet I was hard pressed to recall seeing her wear them. I always folded or ironed the laundry and placed it on the children's beds reminding them to put it away in their closets or dresser drawers.

Tasha often found herself too busy to comply. When she climbed into bed at night the freshly folded clothing "slipped" to the floor and once again became soiled laundry.

When Tasha was in grade seven she took a home economics class. The class included cooking, sewing, laundry and other useful household chores. Home economics class was teaching her to do things that made her feel so grown-up and she loved the class. She had learned how to do laundry the right way and felt no hesitation about correcting my blatant errors. How could I not know that the soap went into the water before the clothing? Now that I was thoroughly trained by an expert in the correct method of doing laundry, Tasha felt that as the trainer she would be the best candidate to do her own laundry.

I agreed, with a few instructions. Experts don't take instruction very well! I told her to use cold water except for whites and to take it easy on the soap. She liked her new freedom and she kept the laundry up-to-date; she occasionally did laundry for her brother and me.

As time went on, I discovered that Tasha would often wash a single pair of jeans and call it a load. She used a full load of hot water and a full cup of detergent; the jeans were then dried for two hours on a hot setting to ensure the perfect shrunkenness. I wondered if she skipped one of her laundry classes. Tasha was often in trouble for her method of laundering a single pair of jeans. Time passed, she grew up and moved away from home.

I had moved away from Alberta. I would occasionally come back to Calgary to visit my girlie pie. On one such occasion I volunteered to do her mountain of laundry that lay in front of the washing machine. She tried to put me off but I insisted on doing it since I had nothing to do all day while she was at work. Finally she agreed to let me do the laundry but not before giving me explicit instructions. We wash everything in cold water except whites; we only use one quarter cup of detergent per load; we only use enough water to properly wash the load. Not everything goes in the dryer. Sweaters are laid flat on towels, bras hang on the towel rod and don't let anything stay in the dryer too long or it wrinkles. Wow, that was all news to me. I'm so pleased that we have a laundry expert in the family.

You always know that your children will grow up some day but it is very strange to be in the same room when it happens.

THE MAGIC WINDOW

On our ranch the most exciting things were seen from the big square kitchen window which overlooked the meadow and the creek. Sometimes it seemed like the window was magical! Every time we looked out, it was essentially the same view yet in some way it was different every time. We spent many exciting hours here with binoculars hoping to catch a glimpse of active weather or any creature that might venture out of the woods.

In the spring we watched the creek waters swell forming a large pond in the lower pasture caused by the snow melt and the spring rains. We saw the swamp come alive with ducks and waterfowl of all varieties as they migrated north. We watched the first geese of spring come squawking in for a landing. We watched the Tree Swallows and the Bluebirds in turn build nests and raise their families. We saw the tall lanky Sandhill Cranes strutting majestically in the meadow. We watched the bald eagles try to sneak up on our young turkeys.

This is where we stood watching the cautious deer wander out of the woods at dusk to graze in the meadow. We watched the wily Coyotes slink conspicuously along the fence line. From here we watched Houston, our little sable Sheltie, frolic with his new friend the small red fox.

We watched in wonder as a lightening-struck tree sent sparks, like fireworks, up into the night sky. We watched as the rain stopped and a beautiful rainbow, often double, would cross the sky seeming to end in our creek. This is where I stood alone paralyzed by fear watching the fog roll in from the creek to sneak up and surround the house. From this window we scanned the meadow for animal tracks in the fresh snow.

We watched Ryan and his cousin Angela skate on the pond after working so hard to clear it of snow. We watched as the farmer brought salt blocks in his truck for his cattle. We watched as hikers, bikers and horseback riders followed the trails through the woods.

During hunting season, it was from here that Larry spotted the moose which he shot from our balcony. From this special window we watched Frisky Lynne, our old lady cat abscond with the baby duck she managed to capture in the highly populated spring swamp. She hurried along the middle rail of the heavy log snake fence followed by the overwrought and very vocal mother duck.

We gazed down the meadow as dozens of Black Angus cows meandered single file along the worn trail to the pond for an evening drink while in the distance the bulls took care of the calves. We could see when the neighbor's pure white Charolais bull escaped his pasture in search of a Black Angus mate or two.

There were always spyglasses hanging at this window. We didn't want to miss a thing. We became so excited any time we saw anything unusual, which was often and we had an urgent need to share the experience with anyone else in the house. We would stomp our feet quietly or whisper loudly to alert others that they were missing something spectacular. We'd share the spyglasses and together marvel at our great good fortune to live in such an extraordinary neighborhood.

THE CONSTRUCTION ZONE

It was our first winter living on the ranch at One Hundred and Fifty Mile House. Larry was away flying helicopter at Esky Creek for several weeks. Ryan was gone to the Fortress Mountain Ski Hill in Kananaskis, Alberta to work for the winter. I wasn't working yet and I needed a project to absorb some of my unbearably lonely and endless leisure time.

Our wonderful log farmhouse had only two bedrooms; both were on the upper level. Ryan liked to sleep in the cooler lower level of the house. Although there was no actual room there he had his bedroom furniture arranged and claimed that space as his bedroom. I so wanted him to have the privacy of a real finished bedroom.

I started to think about what would be needed to build a room and if I would actually be capable of doing this renovation project on my own. After a few days I had it all figured out; I'd have to move the furniture, sand the log beam, tear down and rebuild the problem walls; it was looking possible. The folks at the hardware store and the lumberyard could easily answer any questions that might arise. The only thing that ever held me back from doing anything that Larry could do was brute physical strength and I saw myself as a very strong capable woman. I loved to challenge my skills and I felt confident that I was up to this challenge. After all it was only going to take five or six days working from dawn to midnight every day completely free of interruptions to complete the project.

The initial step was to remove the furniture from the would-be room allowing space to work. I got right at it. All the furniture was moved to the most distant corner of the basement. The furniture was then covered with a tarp to protect it from the inevitable dust that would occur during the sawing and sanding projects.

Next the gray log beam that went all the way across the basement ceiling would have to be sanded. Sanding above my head would be a tough job and stressful on the arms. It took a lot longer than anticipated. I estimated one full day to complete the sanding project but as usual my judgment of the job was off by a great deal. It's like I can only see the big picture and not all the little pieces that make it up. Three weeks later, working intently and continually I had only managed to sand that part of the log that would be visible inside the new bedroom. It was a splendid feature when the sanding was done. There were a couple of large knots in it which created a cozy rustic appearance. It required no finish because it was very attractive on its own. This beautiful log beam would become the front for the open closet.

Pumped to start the walls I went shopping for the building supplies I expected to need. My neighbor Conrad volunteered to transport the goods in his truck because my farm truck was a 1986 Hyundai Pony, a small hatchback car. With the goods on site I started measuring, sawing and building. Soon the closet/laundry room wall was framed in. I had used liquid nail to glue the wood to the cement floor. I was so pleased with my progress, slow though it may have been. Once the frame was built it didn't take long to put the wallboard up to complete that wall.

Next was the inside wall that backed the stairs; I got started at once. It was necessary to remove all the wallboard and replace it. The framework also had to be replaced in order to level the stairs and extend the wall to where the door would be installed. This was the first major glitch in my progress. All the wood used to build this wall was seriously warped. The wall was also an integral part of the stairs. As the wall was dismantled the stairs began to sag. Each step seemed to produce yet another project; not much wonder it was taking so long. I worried about the bucket of worms I had opened. It looked like I may have to re-build the entire house before I was finished. Good thing I started in the basement.

I used a jack-all to raise the sagging stairs into a level position. They had to be held in place while I rebuilt the wall. This wall and the stairs turned out to be a very big job indeed and it was taking much longer than expected. The two-by-fours used to hold the stairs up would have to be replaced with two-by-sixes. Once cut to size they would give the stairs a more secure resting-place and allow for the wall in the bedroom to be perfectly even.

Larry was working at Esky Creek and he would be coming home soon. This part of the job needed to be completed and all the mess cleaned up prior to his return. I almost had a rash worrying about being found out before the six day project already into its sixth week was complete. I could only hope that he would find no reason to go into the basement during his time off.

Wonderful! It snowed hard and Larry was busy catting (plowing) the road most of his two weeks home. He came and went without ever noticing what I was doing in the basement. Well, now that he was gone I could relax and get back to my project.

It was now far beyond the five or six days that I had originally estimated. I easily stepped back in where I had left off prior to Larry's arrival. I worked contemplating the nightmare that might be found in the outside walls.

The outside walls also had been poorly finished. I discovered during the dismantling process that these walls were built without insulation and with poor quality supplies. Both walls had to be replaced completely. I was pleased with all the helpful information received from Revelstoke and Beaver Lumber and with all that I had accomplished. Because every project I completed created another two projects, it didn't seem in the scheme of things that very much had been accomplished yet.

I was busily sanding the window frame when, darn my sandpaper caught a rough edge and tore grinding my progress to a sudden halt. I had plenty of sandpaper to replace it. I just couldn't figure out, in my frustration, how to remove and reapply sandpaper to the belt sander. I didn't want to waste any precious time so I hopped into my farm truck (the Hyundai Pony) and drove over to see if my neighbor could rescue me. Conrad was outside with his brother Rick working on his Cat when I arrived. I asked him to please fix my sander problem. He obliged and I was on my way home without even a visit.

Conrad's road was just over one vehicle width wide during the winter; the sides were heaped with many feet of snow. As I was driving out I met a vehicle driving in. Because I was going up-hill I drove into the snow bank, so the other car could pass me. I would easily be able to back out of the snow bank and be on my way once the other vehicle was past.

As the car neared I turned my head away. I didn't want them to see my dirt and sawdust-covered face. My hat was on backwards, my goggles were on my forehead, there were red goggle lines around my eyes and I looked a mess. They waited for me to turn back to them while they opened their window to talk to me. I was very embarrassed, in a hurry and annoyed that they found it necessary to talk to me when I was making such a deliberate effort to avoid them.

It was Orville Fletcher and his family. In 1926 Orville Fletcher, a Cariboo Pioneer, had apparently lived with his large family in the tiny cottage across the creek from where our house stands today. The family wanted to have one last look at it. The little old house with its sweet-smelling lilacs, broken down corral and dilapidated log snake fence still stand in ruin. It was interesting to meet and chat with a real pioneer but I hoped that my energy level and enthusiasm wouldn't be diminished because of this unforeseen encounter.

At last back at the great home base I got right back into my sanding project. The outside walls would soon be ready for wallboard. Also, it was almost time for Larry to come home and interrupt my progress once again. As keen as I was to continue, I had to get my mess cleared away.

It had snowed heavily once again and thankfully that kept Larry busy catting the road for days. I made sure that there was always something up from the freezer for dinner. I saw to it that there was plenty of wood in for the furnace. I kept my parking area clear of snow. If I were very lucky Larry would again have no reason to go into the basement before returning to Esky Creek.

What a long five or six day stretch this had become. It was already into the fourth month and it was time to resume. I got all the wallboard out and started measuring, cutting and installing. I was moving along quite quickly now. The finishing strips and corners for the wallboard are going up well but darn, I didn't buy enough of them. Anything to interrupt me! How annoying! This would mean another trip to town and a trip to town could mean the loss of a whole day. I often found it necessary to go to town late in the day to ensure that an entire day was not lost to visiting. I'd leave home at four pm.

The closet rod was exactly six feet long which determined the closet length. The wall itself was ten feet six inches long. There would be room for a dividing wall and space to put a chest of drawers. Shelves were installed above the chest so that there was an open cupboard to match the open closet.

It was almost time for Larry to come home again. My five or six days turned into many long months. My project had finally reached completion for my part and it was looking mighty fine.

Larry arrived home from Esky Creek; Ryan arrived home from Fortress Mountain. Both men were very impressed with my secret project. Ryan was thrilled that he finally had his own real bedroom with a door on the basement level of the wonderful log farmhouse.

THE CHICKEN KILLING INVENTION

I raised some chickens for winter meat during that first full summer on the ranch. Now was the time to process the birds before it got too cold outside. They had been pampered little yellow chicks but now they were huge, crippled by their own weight, eating machines. As Murphy's Law would have it this was the same time that Larry would go up north to fly for five or six weeks and Ryan would leave for Kananaskis, Alberta to work on the ski hill for the winter. Alone, by myself, with no one I would have to process all these birds.

Having always been free-range with an automatic feeder, these chickens grew to be an average of eight pounds dressed. They were huge meat birds. Ryan had given some of them names suited to greedy, gimped-up chickens. Due to their size alone, processing would be a problem.

It was not possible for one inexperienced, female, wanna-be farmer to hold the feet together, hold the wings together and cut off the head with the razor sharp hatchet all in a single action. That is of course, unless one had a handy small third arm growing from the chest, an appendage often required to complete ranch chores when alone. I had not yet grown one so I would have to create for myself a chicken killing invention; something to hold the bird securely in place to prevent bruising and tearing, while I committed the dastardly deed.

I was pleased with my creation. It looked a bit mediaeval, yet workable. It was a folded, twisted piece of stucco wire that acted as a wrap. It was nailed to a large fir chopping block. It was held together with a very high-tech bent nail that twisted up to open and down to close.

In theory the high-tech bent nail could be turned up to open the wire, the chicken could be laid on the block, the bird could then be covered with the wire wrap, the nail turned to hold it all together then I could proceed with step two, amputation. It certainly sounded wonderful. Wow! I would have all those chickens processed and in the freezer very quickly.

The invention was complete and ready to test by eleven pm. As a totally result-oriented farmer I couldn't wait until morning to try it out. I must try it right now in the light from the porch. I was proud of my invention and just knew that it would decrease labor and increase production by one hundred percent.

It wasn't hard to sneak up on chickens in the dark of night. They squawked a lot and flapped their wings but they didn't go very far.

At last with an unsuspecting chicken tucked securely under my arm, I made my way to my invention. I twisted the high-tech nail on the chopping block to open the wire wrap. Next I laid the chicken on the block and prepared to cover it with that wrap. This chicken had other evening entertainment ideas, whatever was happening here tonight she wanted no part of. As I turned the nail to close the wire over her body she rebelled. She started flapping around and I had a job keeping her within the confines of the wire wrap.

In my efforts to run one complete test, I felt the wire cut deep into the web between my ring and little finger. I felt the claws of the chicken dig in to rip it further. I instantly administered the only emergency first aid at hand which was to pretend that it hadn't happened. Eventually I emerged victorious. In one hand I held the hatchet and in the other the birds' head. It was an ugly sight, one that could have put me off farming for life if I hadn't been so darn busy and alone. The job was not yet complete; I still had to pluck and cadaver the bird. It had to be wrapped and in the freezer before the night was over. What was I thinking of getting starting so late? Things always happen faster and more incident free in my head than in real life.

In the house I cleaned myself up and prepared for the task ahead. I let the bird sit for a few minutes in hot water to loosen the feathers. It was as I plucked the feathers from the bird that I discovered fresh blood on my hand. A closer look confirmed that it was I who was bleeding. Quite the jagged gash had manifest on that web. It was evident that stitches to close the wound would be in order. Any decision about stitches would have to wait though, because this chicken job had to be completed first.

It was very late when the bird finally made it to the freezer. At this late hour I was not willing to trek off to the Cariboo Memorial Hospital's emergency room, in Williams Lake, for stitches and risk being lost in the dark in the country as well as being wounded. I cleaned the wound and wrapped it. I would administer another dose of emergency first-aid; perhaps I would see a doctor tomorrow.

I was very pleased that I learned all I had about my chicken-killing invention tonight. It would be easier to work with tomorrow in daylight I assured myself. It may need a wee bit of tweaking but the idea was great. I was especially pleased that I had only twenty-three chickens left to process. I took one last look at my chicken killing setup then turned off the porch light.

In spring they were fluffy little chicks. By summer they were very big white chickens, come fall they were crippled by their own weight giants. Alone, by myself, with nobody I found a way to get those birds from the chicken coop to the freezer.

SOUR GRAPES

I saw a lovely wooden basket at the Overwaitea Supermarket while I was grocery shopping. That basket would be perfect for keeping my garden seeds organized. It would be handy to carry while planting the garden and the greenhouse. In order to have that dandy basket I would have to buy the sour little grapes that filled it! After long deliberation I bought the basket of sour grapes at a greater price than I would have liked to pay.

The grapes lasted an exceptionally long time. I offered them to any visitors who happened by. We ate them one grape at a time. They never did seem to go bad and no one really liked them. They sat out on the counter so I would be sure to flog them at every opportunity. I was anxious to have the basket, yet reluctant to throw out food.

One morning I came downstairs to find grapes on the counter and on the floor. I was sure that my cats had been up on the counter so they got a tongue-lashing and were sent outside as punishment. I set several mousetraps that night and placed them strategically around the grapes. The next morning it was the same, grapes on the counter and on the floor again. No traps were sprung during the night, yet I felt sure that the cats had been on the counter again.

This time the cats got a tongue-lashing and were banished to the outdoors for the night.

By the third day I knew there had to be more to it. Both cats were outdoors and there were still grapes on the floor. I looked suspiciously around the room and then I checked the floor and cupboards. Something mysterious was happening in my country kitchen. Finally I pulled the fridge out and looked into the space between the flat back of the counter and the log wall of the kitchen. What a surprise it was to come face to face with a saucy old rat with a large cache of sour little grapes. He was trying to hide from me while defending his hiding place. This was a job for the handy dandy rodent poison and a heart of solid stone.

At last with the saucy old rat and the sour little grapes disposed of, the wooden basket was mine. I could put it to use in the way I had planned from the start, holding and organizing my garden seeds.

WRESTLING MATCH

When I decided to raise a couple of turkeys for Thanksgiving and Christmas, I was advised to purchase at least twenty chicks because the infant mortality rate of turkeys is extremely high. It seemed like a huge price to pay for two turkeys but I really wanted to try my hand raising them. It turned out that I had to purchase twenty four baby birds to get my two. I also had to purchase a brood lamp for my babies. All of my turkeys lived and my friend gave me the six that survived from her original lot. Now I had thirty cute little turkeys growing up. Spring turned to summer and summer to fall. The turkeys got bigger and uglier, in particular the males.

It was now late in the fall and time to get all the turkeys into the freezer. We estimated their average weight to be at least twenty pounds. Ryan and I had to get them slaughtered, plucked and cadavered before it was too cold to work outside. In anticipation of some hard work ahead we both dressed in shorts and t-shirts.

We used a turkey killing technique that had potential. It meant cutting a hole in the bottom of a plastic five-gallon bucket, of which we had many. The trick was to catch the turkey, put the pail over its head and pull the head through the hole in the bottom of the bucket. The bucket would cover the body and protect the wings from damage. It also allowed the turkey to calm down prior to the ugly amputation, ensuring bruise-free tender meat. The only stipulation was that the bird could not exceed twenty-five pounds live. The size was going to be an important factor.

A horrific chase ensued around the farmyard. Countless cuts and scratches later we captured our first turkey. I was lying over the bird to hold it still. It was like fighting a fierce and wild little man. The next dilemma was to get the bucket over its head and body while I was still lying on top of it. Ryan grabbed the bucket and put it over the bird's head. From the bottom end of the bucket he reached through the hole with a gloved hand to grab the turkey's head. It was here that the problems began.

I foolishly loosened my grip on the beast before we discovered that the bucket would be much too small to do the job. It took the total strength of both Ryan and me to hold that critter down. I held the feet together in my hands then tucked them down under my knees. Ryan tightened his grip on the head and he helped me spread the wings on the ground. As Ryan took his first swing with the razor sharp hatchet the terrified bird dug its huge claws into my bare legs. It was his final effort to escape. Three swings of that hatchet later and the head came off in his hand. Ryan and I both lay on top of the struggling turkey until it stopped moving. Although it was rather cool outside, we were both perspiring from the struggle. A cloud of steam was rising up from us into the cooler air.

Only when the bird lay lifeless on the ground did we realize how unexpectedly huge it really was. I couldn't lift it by myself. Ryan hung the bird on the clothesline fifteen feet above the ground to bleed out. The weight of the bird soon pulled the clothesline down to the ground. After we had time to catch our breath Ryan brought that big bruiser to the kitchen where I prepared to pluck, gut and cadaver it.

When the turkeys were ready for the freezer Ryan would step on the bathroom scale to weigh them. This, our first one, weighed a mighty forty-five pounds dressed (without feathers or guts). We lived in mortal fear of the other growing giants still running around! All these creatures would soon have their meeting with the hatchet. We simply couldn't let them get any bigger and they could easily gain pounds per week.

Our great technique to get the turkeys to the freezer became useless due to size but we found a new method, hand to wing combat. It was far less than perfect but it's what we had. We dealt with the males (the ugly looking ones) first since they were already the biggest and still growing. We could only do two in a day. We worked steadily for two more weeks to ensure that those bruisers didn't grow any more and that they all made it to the freezer.

I only wanted a couple of turkeys; one for Thanksgiving and one for Christmas. Who knew that I'd be such an amazing turkey farmer with no mortality rate at all? My amazing turkey farming success can be attributed to patience. Unlike my friend who used the brood lamp to cook her little turkeys at single sandwich stage, I waited until fall to cook mine full grown and able to feed an army.

CAT TRAPS

When we moved to the ranch at One Hundred and Fifty-Mile House we had two adult cats. These cats were very different. One was a charcoal gray, scrawny, spayed female whose name was Frisky Lynn. She was only part Siamese but had inherited the very loud whiney Siamese voice. She would never allow anyone to ignore her. When she started to meow with that Siamese accent and bunt us with her head, we were forced to acknowledge her. She was a good little cat coming when she was called, asking to go out and not hanging around the table at mealtime.

The second cat was a big orange neutered tomcat named Tony Balogna. He was the same age and of no special breeding. Tony was rather aloof. He would do anything asked of him, whenever he felt like it. His voice was decidedly masculine, very deep with a short quiet meow. He too was a very good cat coming when he was called, asking to go out and not hanging around the table at mealtime.

These kitties were just what we liked in a cat. Prior to our move to the Fifty they were both accustomed to finding their food up on a high shelf safe from the dog. Now with the move their food was under the stairs and again safe from the dog. They didn't bother to jump up anymore, not on the table and not on the counter. We were proud of them.

Anytime we left anything on the counter that might tempt our good little kitties, we covered it with a huge bowl. One night the bread was left out on the counter uncovered and in the morning there was a hole in the bag and part of a few slices were nibbled. We started being suspicious after that and we would listen for our dear kitties as soon as the lights were turned out. Who was teaching who these bad habits? Now bread on the counter now chicken scraps in the bucket! We would have to pay closer attention.

Larry went to work up north for several weeks. I decided to gather up all the mousetraps I could find in the house. When I was ready to go to bed I set the mousetraps and placed them on the counter and in the sink. I went to bed followed by two model cats that made themselves comfortable on the foot of the waterbed. I lay in bed a long while waiting for them to make their move. When the cats didn't leave the bed I began thinking I was wrong about them. Maybe there was a dreaded rat in the house again!

Almost asleep, I felt the waterbed move as one of the model cats slinked quietly to the floor, soon after the other cat followed. I lay awake listening.

Suddenly the house was alive. Mouse traps were snapping and surprised cats were jumping to the floor. Neither cat made a sound; their voices would have given them away. Both my very good cats were being very bad. Drifting off to sleep I felt both my humiliated kitties slink back onto the foot of the waterbed.

In the morning there were sprung traps strewn about. The mousetraps were used every once in a while to keep the cats in line. Still years later, we would occasionally hear the snap of a mousetrap and the sound of surprised kitty feet hitting the floor as some foolish kitty was testing fate once again.

PET RAT

Our cozy log farmhouse, built by two women, had some major construction flaws. One flaw in particular made this house especially appealing to the country critters every year come fall. There was a ten-inch gap under the full length of the bottom log at the east and west sides of the house. This opening was hidden on the outside by the full deck on both sides of the house and on the inside by the wallboard on the apparently finished wall.

Ryan had been downstairs in bed for a while when I retired myself. I fell to sleep at once and I started dreaming. Startled, I realized that the sound I was hearing was not a part of my dream; it was Ryan downstairs shouting me to "come quick." I hurried as fast as I could in the dark, down the stairs to his room on the lower level.

There perched on a post in Ryan's bedroom sat a....well.... hmmm.... what the heck is it? At first sight we thought it was a chinchilla. We had seen a pet chinchilla in the past and this creature did look like a chinchilla. Maybe it's a packrat! I heard that packrats smell and this creature didn't smell. We stared at it and it stared back at us. It didn't seem to be as afraid as it had been and neither were we as afraid of it. As time passed we decided to get the encyclopedias out and look for the creature. We determined that it must be a trade rat. They were common in our area. After a while Ryan came to like the creature that didn't seem to want to leave his room.

I went upstairs to get the rodent poison and traps. When I returned Ryan said that he wanted to keep the rat as a pet. The answer is "no" Ryan. However cute we may think he is we can not have a rat as a pet. With that settled the rodent poison and traps were set out.

Built by two women, the flaws of this house were hidden rather than eliminated. Next fall the appeal of a warm home for country critters would not exist thanks to chinking and finishing, the two critical log home construction steps that the ladies neglected.

THE ROAD FROM HELL

In spring the road from hell was a winding, hilly, deeply rutted five point two kilometers of rock-infested mud soup. It was barely passable in four-wheel drive when it was wet. There had been mega-tons of gravel laid on the road but it didn't take long for all that to be devoured by the voracious mud. It would take years of constant heavy gravel application to build up a base and satisfy the insatiable appetite of that mud.

The road was often not car-worthy. I wouldn't drive my car in for weeks or months at a time. I parked my car in Borland Valley at a house on the paved road, near the entrance to the road from hell. I'd four by four or walk in and out those long kilometers while the road was impassable.

It was spring and in the spring the entire road was rock and mud soup from spring thaw and run off. Walking that stretch was quite the survival adventure. My neighbor, Debbie and I were out on the road every day in the spring repairing ruts that fun-seekers left with their off road vehicles and attempting to drain the surface water to help speed drying.

Apparently I was being sent a message to inform me of a death in the family from my sister in Winnipeg. I had not had contact with her for several years and she didn't know very much about my current status. My mailing address was a box number. The telephone was an autotel, the number unlisted. The Williams Lake RCMP was delivering this message. Automobile registration, which had been changed from Alberta to BC only one day previous, was used to track me down.

The search indicated that I could be located in Borland Valley at One Hundred and Fifty-Mile House. The officers took the scenic thirty minute drive to the country. By nine o'clock pm my car was located in Borland Valley at a neighbor's home on Eagle Way. When Ruth was questioned about my car, she told the officers that she didn't even know me, that I just parked there because our road was not car-worthy. She pointed out our road and the fact that I lived at the very end of it. She told them also that they would require four by four to gain entry. The officers had a look at the sloppy mess that we fondly referred to as our road. They promptly returned to the Williams Lake base for a more suitable vehicle to complete their assignment.

It was after ten o'clock at night. I had been in bed reading for a while already. My faithful companion Houston was lying near the bed as I set my book aside and turned the light off. I fell to sleep at once only to be awakened by Houston's quiet Grrrrr. I called him up onto the bed where he tuckled beside me; again he Grrred. I hugged him close but he kept on Grrrring. It seemed he knew something I didn't know.

By the time that I realized someone actually was there, I could hear voices approaching. I leaped out of bed and raced down the stairs, past the front door to the gun rack. Grabbing my rifle from the rack, I hastily loaded it in the dark. I couldn't see anything out the window. There was no moon or stars so it was very dark outside. This was my first time to be frightened in the country.

Footsteps on the front step, a knock on the door! I held my breath. Male voices called my name. They identified themselves as RCMP officers and asked that I open the door. I refused to open up and asked in the deepest voice I could conjure up what they wanted. They said that they wanted to talk to me. I turned on the deck light and asked them to step over near the window to show me their identification. They did. I peeked out through the closed Venetian blinds to see their badges but still didn't open the door. They relayed the message they had came to deliver. I thanked them then bid them good night. Making sure that all the thick, homemade doors with slide latches were locked, I shelved my rifle and went back to bed.

From my bedroom I could hear them slosh out to their vehicle. I heard their motor rev and tires spin as they tried to turn around in the muck and mire. Slowly they would slip and slide in the rock soup which made up the road from hell, until they reached the pavement of Borland Valley Estates at One Hundred and Fifty Mile House, BC.

FOR THE LOVE OF A BLUEBIRD

I saw a family of bluebirds along our driveway. They had come closer and closer until at last they were at my house trying to build a nest in the rafters. I wanted them to stay but not in the rafters! Bluebirds were new to me and I liked them a lot. They were pretty to look at and they made a pleasant sound.

Buster Ellison, my old friend, told me that if I built simple little wooden birdhouses for the bluebirds they would come and they would use them. He said to put the houses up on the fence posts in twos. He said that the tree swallows would use one house and the bluebirds would use the one next door. The tree swallows would arrive earlier and they would be gone before the bluebirds arrived. It sounded like a tall tale to me, something that an old man might tell a child. Buster said that he had some of these small bird-houses on his far fence and sent me out to have a look at them.

I so wanted the bluebirds to come live at my house. Even though I didn't truly believe Busters' story I asked Larry to build six of those little bird houses just in case. Four were put on tall extensions then nailed onto fence posts near the house. I wanted to be able to look out the kitchen window, or the magic window as it came to be known, to see the bluebirds if they really came. The other two houses went on tall extensions on the fence beside the garden. The extensions were necessary to protect the birds from Tony Balogna and Frisky Lynn the curious and apparently hungry resident cats. When spring arrived I started my Bluebird vigil.

I was sure that it wouldn't happen as the old man said. I watched and patiently waited. To my amazement the Tree Swallows came and moved into; imagine that, every other house! The swallows built their nests, laid their eggs and raised their young. When the babies were all grown they were taught to fly and soon they were all gone.

Time passed. I kept an ever-watchful eye on the vacant birdhouses. I had noticed bluebirds in the area looking for a home. At last, there was a pair on the barbed wire fence checking out the vacant little houses. In turns the bluebirds popped in and out of the houses. Ahhh, they approved! They started at once to build their nest. In and out they went with sticks, feathers, puppy hair, grass and any other soft building material that they found. The next day another pair arrived. After they examined the other house thoroughly the second family of bluebirds moved in and they too began building a nest. A third family moved into the little house near the garden.

The bluebird families worked from dawn to dusk to get their nests finished in time for the arrival of their young. I kept an ever-watchful eye throughout the summer. From the window and through binoculars, I was able to see into the houses. I watched as the females laid their eggs. I watched as the eggs hatched. I watched as the parent birds, in turn, brought food for their ever-starving, very vocal young. It was positively thrilling.

At this particular time the bluebird babies were maturing, almost ready to leave the nest. Most of their time was spent near the door now and they were increasingly vocal. I patiently waited to see the young test their wings.

I was in my house when I heard Houston barking under a tree near the house. Houston was the squirrel guard. After we got them out of the rafters no squirrel was allowed on our log house or in the seven trees surrounding it. A squirrel must be in one of those seven trees. From the window I could see a great commotion involving a squirrel, a dog and a bluebird. I went outside to further investigate. Once outside, it became clear that a wretched squirrel was not just in one of those seven trees but it was threatening the bluebird babies. Houston was barking at the squirrel and the Momma bluebird was loudly defending her young. This looked like a job for the trusty twenty two. I hurried into the house to fetch and load it.

When I returned to the scene it was with a loaded rifle and a heart of solid stone. I determined that the squirrel simply had to go. It had an entire forest to find adventure and food. There was no need for it to be in one of my seven trees, especially threatening my baby bluebirds.

Not to say I was a poor shot or anything but it took seven shots for me to put an end to the battle. Houston got his squirrel and the bluebird babies were safe once more. When the drama was over, the mother bluebird fluttered close to my face chirping. I know that she was saying, "thank-you for saving my family!"

The next morning I got up early and checked the bluebird houses straight away. There were no young to be seen in either nest. I felt sure that another squirrel came by and got them before I woke up. It made me feel very sad. I tried to protect them!

Some birds came swooping across the pasture to rest on the barbed wire fence beneath the little wooden birdhouses. It was the two bluebird families come to say good-bye. One family had two female offspring the other had two males and one female. They were all safe now; they could fly.

CHUMMING FOR BARRACUDA

In 1990 we went to Cancun, Mexico for a winter holiday. It is a fantastic place to holiday and the best place ever to buy silver. I purchased several pieces which I wore all the time. I got a necklace, two bracelets and an anklet.

From Cancun we took the bus to Chatamul, the border city between Mexico and Belize. Here we changed to Central America's Batty Bus Line. We went immediately through customs and then on to Belize City. The terrain changed as we left Chatamul, from dense jungle to wide open sugar cane fields. It was a very uncomfortable ride from the border. If you didn't have a huge sense of adventure it would have been no fun at all. The seats in the Batty bus were completely worn out; some had springs poking through. My seat had a huge hole in the center and was slanted to one side; it was much like sitting on a three-legged commode for several hours.

I didn't speak any of the local languages so I was suspicious of all Mexicans, Mayans and Belizians. Protecting my luggage with my life, I held my backpack on my lap for most of the trip. We arrived in Belize City just before dark.

How pleased I was to get off that commode. We took a taxi to the first hotel we came to. After checking in and having dinner in their dining room, we checked our valuables (American cash, visa cards and jewelry in a brown paper bag) with the desk clerk. The desk clerk, who also wore the chef's hat tossed the bag on the counter behind his workstation.

We left the building and went for a walk in the darkness of the uncivilized night time Belize City. Belize is a very poor country and people say that it's not safe there for gringo tourists to walk the streets alone at night. Most of these warnings seemed over-emphasized and we decided to live on the edge. We were planning to hike a couple of blocks to the docks.

On our walk we met a tall young black Belizian man who did his best to extort money from us. We didn't play his game. He stayed with us back to the hotel where we bought him a meal and talked a while. We soon went to our rooftop abode and the young man was removed from the restaurant.

Safely back at our cockroach-infested penthouse suite we sat on the edge of the roof, without railings, and watched the action in the streets three floors below. It gets dark at about six o'clock pm in Belize due to its proximity to the equator. We had a very long and exciting evening of people-watching from our rooftop perch high above the streets.

In the morning we dressed, had breakfast and collected our valuables. The clerk/cook took the bag from the counter where he had put it last night. It was intact. We stepped out into a different, much more civilized, daytime Belize City.

Our packs on our backs, we window-shopped as we made our way to the boat launch. We had to find Chocolate, a weathered little Belizian man who would take us in his boat to the small island of Caye (key) Caulker. We would make it our home for the next two weeks.

As we skimmed over the perfectly clear water en route to the Island, we saw dolphins traveling in large groups. The dolphins leaped in and out of the water just doing what dolphins do in a day. I found myself very curious to know what exactly it was that dolphins do in a day. We also saw rays that could leap ten feet out of the water and appear to be flying. Chocolate told us that these rays sometimes spring out of the water and land in unsuspecting boats, which makes for a very exciting trip. In the water there were lobster pots marked by tall poles. Many species of unique and colorful tropical fish in various shapes and sizes made their home along the reef. Large Conch shells could be seen on the sandy floor of the crystal clear coral reef.

On the small island of Caye Caulker we found a place to stay as soon as we arrived. It was a small newly-built, almost-finished cabin on stilts feet from the beach. What a lucky find!

Some areas of beach were nicer than others and it didn't take long to find the best spot. The Cut was a narrow stretch where the Island of Caye Caulker had been ripped in half by a fierce hurricane in 1988. The sand was pure white; the water was clear and deep. We went swimming there quite often and today I went alone.

There were many tourists and locals swimming at The Cut so I decided to swim in the sea. I had my snorkel gear and was enjoying the wonderful underwater view when I felt watched. I surfaced briefly but didn't notice anyone suspicious so I went back underwater. Again I had that feeling in the pit of my stomach. This time I turned slowly in a huge circle underwater. I almost gasped when I saw it. A barracuda looking me in the eye or was it my shiny necklaces, bracelets and anklet that he was eyeing up? When I am scared I remember very big. I believe that fish was of record-breaking size. *Barracuda are thin fish up to five and a half feet long, attracted to shiny objects moving in the water. They have been known to attack people in the Atlantic Ocean.* (World Book Encyclopedia). Thank goodness I was in the Caribbean Sea however, I wasn't sure that the barracuda could tell the difference.

I cautiously backed away to shallow water keeping my eye on the giant fish. I didn't enjoy swimming there so much after that experience. No one seemed to empathize when they heard my story. Most locals said that with all that jewelry dangling from my body it looked like I was chumming (putting out bait) for barracuda.

A winter holiday in Mexico and Central America is an awesome adventure. Take along a smile, lots of American cash, take a huge sense of adventure and watch out for those big fish.

SKELETON NEST

Once again it was the fall of the year. I was busy neating (cleaning) up the yard, the flower garden, the vegetable garden and my wonderful log greenhouse preparing them for spring. I went around the yard to collect any tools that may have been left out. I wanted everything to be neat before the first dump of snow came. I left the woodshed and my shed, in which I stored building supplies and other miscellaneous items, for my last project and now it was that time.

There was loose hay in one corner of my crowded shed. I couldn't get at it easily. I worked around things the best I could. The tools were hung on the wall. The boxes were put on the shelves. I stacked the plywood pieces and full sheets against the wall and called it good.

A few days later Houston started barking at the door of my shed and he wouldn't stop. He was seriously bothered by something in there. My first thought was that a dreaded squirrel was in my shed annoying him. Certainly there was something that didn't belong there. I carefully checked through the shed. I was moving one sheet of plywood at a time when I came face to face with a large trade rat. It wasn't huge but it was big enough. It was cheeky, it was a rat and it was in my shed. I wanted it out and to that end

I went at once for the rodent poison. The poison kills the critter and causes it to dehydrate entirely.

I didn't want my pets to die so I took special care that the dogs and cats were not out prowling at night while the poison was out and I had to hide the rodent poison from my critters during the day. After a few days most of the rat poison was gone and Houston seemed to lose interest in my shed. I was pleased because I was sure I had rid us of another rat.

When spring finally arrived I was again out neating up the yard and the woodshed area. It's always a mess after winter. There was bark, sticks, hay, and feathers and now I noticed bits of sheepskin from the motorbike seat. I raked all the bits up into a pile and threw them into the wheelbarrow. I was looking forward to having a fire later. There was still a piece of sheepskin under the wall dividing the woodshed from the shop and I was having a problem getting it out. With a strong little stick I poked at it until it loosened and I was able to pull it out.

Sheepskin, hay, grass, hair and feathers all woven together, it looked like a nest of some sort. It was lightweight. My curiosity was aroused; this warranted a much closer look.

With glove clad hands I carefully opened the tangle of woven bits. WOW! It is a nest, a rat nest! There inside, curled up in the fetal position, was the perfect and perfectly clean skeleton of a rat. It occurred to me that this must be the remains of the unfortunate rat I met while neating up my shed last fall.

ON THE EDGE

It was the 90-91 ski season at Fortress Mountain. All of Ryan's friends would be working there for the winter. Jason, his good friend from school would be there for sure, not to mention all the new lifties (young people working the ski lifts) he would meet. I knew that it would be a grand adventure for Ryan to be working on the ski hill, snowboarding during his time off. I would miss him but I was happy that he was going. He needed a grand adventure.

You just don't know adventure until you go on one with Ryan. If the adventure had to be dreamed up, Ryan would be the dreamer. If he had to go hunting for one, he would hunt until one was found. If someone had to risk life and limb, it would be Ryan. For this reason he was nicknamed "The Master of Disaster" when he was six years old. Ryan is the adventure king. In the wilderness of Fortress Mountain he would have no problem finding grand and extreme adventures.

Out the back door of his condo was a very steep slope; it was hard to judge distance with all the big trees. Ryan, Jason and Mike accepted this very steep, heavily treed slope as a direct challenge to their survival skills. To increase the excitement they started out after work, after dark and probably on an empty stomach. Fortunately it was a mild spring evening with a temperature of plus five to plus ten degrees.

It was tough terrain, awkward to snowboard or even to walk for that matter. Making their way downward to the river for two or three hours already, Mike finally gave up his skis. The trio stayed on the same side of the open river until they reached the bridge. What a relief it was for them to see that bridge and know that they made it to highway forty. As they walked they were pleased to see the familiar little grocery store. They banged on the door of the store and made a lot of noise hoping to arouse anyone sleeping therein. No one answered the distress call. The boys had exerted a lot of energy by now. They had walked a long way and were feeling very cold and very tired.

Back on highway forty hiking to the Fortress Mountain ski hill, encouraging one another to keep going; they saw the headlights of a vehicle which they unanimously decided to flag down. The motor home occupants were on the way to a ski weekend at Fortress. They were willing to take the three exhausted adventurers up the hill to their great home base. Gratefully the boys climbed aboard.

After their seven-hour hike the trio arrived home at midnight. They were glad to be home. Hill management was making arrangements with search and rescue to begin a search in the morning. The trio arrived just in time to have the search and rescue plans cancelled and to climb into their warm beds.

Ryan was pleased to be working at Fortress Mountain for the 1990-91 ski seasons. He and his friends were expecting to live on the edge and to have some grand adventures. Who knew that with Ryan and his friend's grand and life threateningly dangerous would be interchangeable verbs to describe their style of adventure?

VERTIGO

It was about five pm when Ryan and I set out for a ride on our motorbikes. We would travel the five point two kilometers to the end of our road and on the way back we'd pick up any litter thrown out by hunters or people who just didn't care. We did this regularly so that people would not see litter along the way and hopefully, would not be as inclined to toss litter out of their vehicles onto our road.

I usually let Ryan take the lead because he was a much better and much faster rider than I. Sometimes he would let me go ahead and be the leader, a position I rarely held on my own. I took advantage of the opportunity he presented and went as fast as I could go on my little red CT 110.

The road was lined with tall trees and seemed quite dark. As I negotiated a turn in the road the setting sun came through the trees creating a vertigo effect. Unable to see where I was going, I didn't know if I was still on the road or off in the woods. The road was so bad that it was hard to tell even when I could see. I thought I had corrected but I wasn't sure.

I hit a large rock and now in my mind I had become a cartoon character. I was flying in a small plane like the Red Baron. I was in and out of trees, over and under bridges; I squeezed through power lines doing loop-de-loops and flips. Suddenly I crashed to a halt in my little aircraft and I was no longer a cartoon character.

I could hear Ryan calling to me, "Are you alright mom?" I was lying on my back on rocks, barely aware of what had just happened, yet starting to feel the pain of it. Ryan was by my side. He tried to help me up but the pain was too great. He would have to go for help. Ryan was afraid to leave me alone because of wild animals, yet he knew that he had to get help. Before he left me he pulled my long hair down over my face to protect me from the swarms of mosquitoes.

The diagnosis of that incident was two crushed vertebrae. It took four months and hundreds of Tylenol III to get past the pain. I still ride my motorbike but I have a much greater respect for speed and for vertigo.

I am willing to forego any opportunity that would place me in the lead. I like to travel slowly on that road so I can see where I'm going, take time to adjust my eyes to the vertigo and stay on the road.

GO HOUSTON!

Houston was a fourteen-year-old sable Sheltie. He had lived with us for thirteen of those fourteen years as the youngest member of the family. Houston is totally dedicated to protecting his master and his yard. He would trot down to the creek for a drink but he always rushed right back to protect his house. It's the nature of a Sheltie

I was looking out the kitchen window or the magic window as it came to be known when I saw a most unusual sight. Houston was tearing across the small pasture in pursuit of what looked like a large orange cat. Though he couldn't hear me I cheered him on. "Go Houston, get that cat out of here!" I shouted. Stray animals in the country often bring disease to domestic country pets. In just a split second Houston was on his way back only this time the cat was chasing him! Is that a cat? They ducked under the fence and leaped across the creek running as fast as they could. As they neared the house I saw that the cat chasing him was not a cat at all but a small Red Fox. I reached for my spyglasses to get a better look at them. Oh my! Houston was frolicking in the pasture with a small red fox. As I watched they ran in huge circles in the pasture, now fox after dog, now dog after fox. Happily they ran along leaping the creek and ducking the fence, their long coats rippling in the wind.

Fox and Coyote often play with domestic dogs giving them a false sense of security as they lure the domestic animals away to the woods, sometimes for the purpose of breeding, sometimes as a source of food. Houston was an old neutered male and that left very little question as to their purpose.

Though I thought it was cute to see Houston frolic with his new playmate, the little red fox, I knew the danger. I needed my Houston here to protect me. I got my rifle out and fired a few shots into our target pit to scare the fox away. He scurried for the woods in double time. Houston appeared disappointed when his friend ran away in the midst of their game. He was not interested in following the little red fox but seemed content to resume protecting his master, his house and his yard.

DOUBLE-HEADER

It must be fall in the Cariboo. There are sounds in the walls again. The sounds of small critters getting ready for winter! I really thought that with two adult cats in the house I wouldn't have this quandary. In the country there are a lot of mice and perhaps my cats had tired of their fair weather diet of moles and mice over the summer. It was a worry to have a mouse in the house knowing how even one mouse can do so much damage.

It appeared that tonight I would have to set my many mousetraps and catch that little rascal. Between the cats and the mousetraps the intruders didn't have a chance.

In our house it was wise to wear slippers when getting out of bed at night. Even with lights on a groggy and sleepy mind might not notice a present from the favorite kitties awaiting them at the foot of the stairs, until it was stepped on with bare feet.

A springing trap woke me from my sleep and I got up to go investigate. I was more asleep than awake as I made my way down the stairs to where I heard the springing trap. As I reached the main level my foot curled up in shock. I had forgotten my very own important rule, to put my slippers on. I was standing on an unwanted gift that the cats had brought for my approval. I just hate it when that happens!

My journey in the darkness continued; I was much more awake now. I turned on a light and began checking the traps. They all seemed to be baited and set but I knew I heard one spring shut. I went into the bathroom to dispose of the first mouse in the toilet when I saw an amazing thing. There was one trap capturing two mice. One mouse was incoming and one was outgoing when the trap sprung.

It was pleasing to be rid of three mice in one night. It was even more pleasing to find a double-header, two mice in one trap. It may have been their very great good fortune to find a cozy warm farmhouse for the winter, but two cats and many traps can make short work of the good fortune of an unwanted country mouse.

COLLISION

It was the end of August just days before his birthday when I went to Vancouver to visit my sister. Ryan didn't want to miss any soccer games so he remained at the great home base. We lived at the end of the mud road from hell, over five kilometers off the paved roads of Borland Valley at One Hundred and Fifty Mile House. Ryan didn't have a car although he was not hurting for transportation. He had his **XL** 175 motor bike that took him over any terrain at breakneck speeds.

His friend had volunteered to pick him up for the soccer games and to drive him home after. Steve had a new car that he didn't want to drive over our ugly road; he asked Ryan to ride out on his motorbike to meet him at the end of it. Ryan packed his things in a bag, swung the bag onto his back, donned his helmet and screamed away from home on his motorbike. He would park his bike at Kim's house which was the first house on pavement at the end of our road.

The soccer game was won and Ryan was dropped off at our road just as dark was closing in. Without changing into biking clothes he put on his helmet, swung the bag onto his back and hastened to be home before dark. He was traveling scarily fast; dust rooster tailing high in his wake. He was tearing around the dangerous hairpin turns, past the swamp, down the hill and then, well, Ryan was waking up on the ground in complete darkness wondering whatever had happened.

When he came to, he could hear his motorbike sputtering as it lay on its side. He knew that he would have to stand the bike upright or it would stall. He started to rise and found himself to be in a great deal of pain. What the heck happened to me? How did I get here?

The headlight on the bike was shining off into the night woods. Out of the corner of his eye Ryan could see the probable cause of his pain. Boasting a mighty rack of antlers, a huge moose peered menacingly at him from the woods. It appeared that this moose would challenge him while he was at such a great disadvantage. Tightly in the grip of fear he questioned what to do now? Should he run to the woods to get away or make a lot of noise and hope to frighten that bruiser away? Running to the woods was out of the question. He was lying on the ground in terrible pain unable to move. He opted to make a lot of noise and the moose slowly turned and casually trotted into the night woods.

There were still three kilometers to go on that very rough road to reach the safety of the great home base; if he could even get up. It was now very dark and he felt very much alone yet watched.

It was a struggle to get up. The wind had been knocked clean out of him. Every part of his body was sore. The motorcycle was still running thank goodness, but the handlebars were twisted forty-five degrees. Considering the pain he was feeling right now pushing the bike or walking would not be options. He tried to straighten the handlebars but he just didn't have the strength. He climbed aboard and struggled to ride home. Every bump in the road was exaggerated a hundred times and taking its toll on his already bruised and shaken body. It was a very long, slow, bumpy three kilometers to the medicine cabinet, a hot bath and safety.

Later on the telephone he relayed his story to me saying, "I always wanted to see a moose close up but, WOW that was a bit too close!" We often did run into moose on our road but not usually literally as Ryan did.

The country, what an amazing, exciting and sometimes dangerous place to live, particularly alone!

BEAR SCARE

I met a man in my neighborhood with two Clydesdale/Shire horses. The heavy horses were in a fairly small pasture; Harold had to feed hay all year because there was no grass left in the pasture. I, on the other hand, had a quarter section of grass and no horses at all. As he had more horses than pasture and I had more pasture than horses, he agreed to bring Jock and Molly to stay for a while at my acreage.

It was nice to have the horses around. They ate the grass, drank from the creek and enjoyed the space they had to run around in. I enjoyed the adventure of having them there. Over the fence I gave each one a handful of oats daily to insure that they would come to me when I called them.

Late on this particular afternoon I couldn't see the horses. It was more that I sensed they were missing. They had some hiding places heavily treed with poplars; here they would hide from the clouds of flies and mosquitoes that monopolized the summer air in Cariboo Country. I went hiking in the pasture to have a look for them. I called out their names as I shook the bucket of oats I carried to tempt them out of the hiding place. In the end I walked the full perimeter of the property through swamp, bush, rocks, creek and long grass all except for a short stretch of about forty feet.

I thought that perhaps Harold had taken his horses away for some reason so I telephoned him to find out. Harold said that he hadn't taken Jock and Molly and would come right over to help me look for them. I told Harold of my search around the perimeter and that I would go down the meadow on my motorbike to have a look.

Quickly I gassed up my CT-100 trail bike and proceeded through the first gate, across the pasture and over the bridge. As I arrived at the second gate that would access the meadow, I noticed a big Black Angus bull standing around too close for my comfort. Being afraid of bulls and realizing that a smart bull would recognize that fear in me I waited until he left before I took down the rails to sneak through the gate. Rails replaced, I started my bike and sped along the fence. I sneaked around the dilapidated little old house, the former home of Cariboo pioneer Orville Fletcher and his family. I sped past the log corral successfully avoiding that massive bull, whose whereabouts I checked on before proceeding into the open meadow. It appeared that the black devil had already lost interest in me and was rolling happily in a dirt hole.

I turned away and started my bike again. Revving the motor, I tore down the trail and into the open meadow. To my horror a big black bear was coming in my direction from the swamp across the meadow. The bear looked up and saw me at the same time I saw him. Ah oh! I'm on the same side of the fence as a live, wild and running Black Bear. So what that he was now running the other way! In my terror my mind became a complete blank, void of all previous motorbike driving skills. I had stalled the bike and I couldn't take the time to re-learn anything. I had to run for my life. I was in the same meadow and on the same side of the fence as a live bear. In my fright and flight I almost bulldozed over that big Black Angus bull as I struggled to reach my own side of the barbed wire fence and safety.

Jock and Molly were later found a few feet outside the fence. A small stretch of fence was down in those forty feet between where I started and ended my perimeter search. I was pleased that my new friend Harold was there to help bring them back because as I discovered, I am also afraid of frisky young Clydesdale/Shire horses.

THE THREE LITTLE PIGS

It was August when our neighbor purchased the three little pigs he would raise over winter. He had a wonderful log pen to keep them in; there was even a little house for them to sleep in at night. Those pigs would be plenty big by winter to withstand the harsh Cariboo weather. Conrad was so pleased that the meat-growing process had begun; he even thought he could smell the bacon cooking.

The morning after the piglet's arrival we were awakened by some unusual noises. We didn't bother to look out because it could have been anything and would likely be long gone by the time we got up to look. Soon after, we heard familiar voices that did get our attention. It was our neighbors and we put the coffee on for them. They didn't really have time for coffee, they explained; the three little pigs had escaped from their new home and they wondered if we had seen them. We thought about the strange noises heard earlier that morning and wondered if it had been them.

When living in the country and the neighbor is in trouble there is an unwritten law that one must lend a hand no matter how one may feel about the other. Quickly we all dressed for a pig hunt in the woods. We poured a to-go cup of coffee for each person in the search party and were on our way.

Debbie and Conrad walked through the bush on either side of the road, Ryan and his friend Jason walked cross-country through the woods and I took the scenic route to come up from the back end of the property. We banged sticks and shouted as we made our way toward the open pig-pen. We could all be heard in the distance shouting "Over here!" or "Here they come!" The three little pigs ran so close together that they looked like a single very weird animal. Around and around the property they ran, through bush, marsh, creek and fences. We were all starting to get tired and we hoped that those dreaded little pigs were tiring also.

Conrad went into the pigpen to put some food in a bucket for the trio. He shook the bucket hoping to lure the three elusive little escapees back into their pen with the familiar sound. The little pigs sniffed around the entrance as five of us closed in on them. For no obvious reason, all three turned and ran in different directions and we were back into the woods pig hunting once again.

It was strange to see those little pigs in the wild. They looked silly and naked running in the woods. They didn't suit that environment at all, although I have known of pigs that ran with the cows for their entire lives.

A few more trips around the woods and alas they were wearing down. Reluctantly they made their way to the only place in the woods where they knew they'd find food, water and rest. We quickly sealed off their escape route from the inside and outside. Those little critters wouldn't escape from that weak area again as it became the strongest part of the pigpen.

In a few short hours we went from starting the meat growing process, to losing the piglets, to saving the bacon. All is well in the 160 acre woods.

ALIEN LIGHTS

Ryan was home alone on the ranch. He wasn't usually nervous on his own because we had a variety of guns for protection and he could handle any one of them. Anyway, who in their right mind would come out to the wilderness in the dark of night? Ryan slept in the walkout basement. He was on his way to his room in the darkness when he glanced out the window and saw a light in the meadow across the creek.

Someone was coming toward our house with a flashlight. Who would be out there at this time of night? The light would go off and then on again. Sometimes it would go off in one place and come back on in another. Uh Oh! There was more than one light. Ryan could handle one on one easily, but how many were out there and who were they?

There seemed to be a lot of lights now. Ryan sneaked out the back door to get a better look and to listen for any noise that would give him a clue. Ducking down behind the cement wall, he peeked over now and then to see if they were any closer. He could hear nothing but the sounds of insects.

In the light of the quarter moon, he looked around to find a place to run away from the house if they kept coming toward him. There were lights by the fire pit, by the woodpile and there were lights by the outhouse. He knew now that he was completely surrounded and seriously outnumbered so he hurried back into the house and locked the door. He watched through the window awaiting the inevitable attack.

He felt silly, quite embarrassed, yet a flood of relief when he realized that those alien lights were everywhere and made no sound because they were nocturnal insects. This would be his first ever encounter with fireflies.

BEARS

Tasha was visiting at the ranch which was always an exciting time for both of us. She loves a good adventure as long as it doesn't scare her. She always hoped to see some wild animal close up, maybe even a bear, but anytime we to were in a position where this was a possibility she would be too frightened. Like her mom she doesn't want to be on the same side of the fence as a wild animal. She would prefer to be in a car with a big gun in her hand.

There were some great logging roads through the agricultural lease that surrounded our ranch. We would walk the logging roads closing all the gates we opened. When we came out to the meadow, we'd cross over to the five mile hay field and make our way back home through that very tall hay. The trip distance was about four kilometers, an excellent workout for the body and a wonderful adventure walk.

I carried my rifle because we could meet with any kind of danger in the woods. Not that I could shoot anything but at least I could make a loud noise to frighten anything to scary away. I felt very courageous with my rifle in hand. Tasha and I chattered on as we walked casually along the trail checking out wild flowers, changing leaves, rushing creeks, lakes along with fish and birds unique to the area.

As we neared the meadow, Tasha saw something black through the trees. Her imagination shifted into high gear. She started to run away. "It's a bear," she shouted, "Run for your life mom!" I couldn't see a bear so I kept looking and asking where she saw it. "Run!" she shouted. Had my girl forgotten that I carried the rifle with which to frighten wild animals away? All I could see were the dozens of Black Angus cattle in the meadow up yonder. They were the cattle that actually lived in this field. These cattle were laying down relaxing, chewing their cud in the coolness of the woods.

Our adventure walk was over for today. It would take some time for Tasha to recover from her encounter with the cows, possibly until her next visit. She'll work hard to build up the courage needed to go back out looking for adventure in the wilds of One Hundred and Fifty Mile House.

THE PERFECT TREE

I usually had my tree up and decorated long before Christmas. This year the kids were coming. I wanted them to help in the hunt for the perfect tree. It wasn't especially cold that winter of 1993 and there was very little snow on the ground. The children had come from Calgary to spend Christmas with us at the ranch and they wanted snow. At first they were disappointed by the lack of it but then the heavens opened up. Enough huge snowflakes fell that it was necessary to plow the road five times in one day.

Tasha went with me in the Blazer to find the perfect Christmas tree as we once again plowed the road. We drove slowly up and down the tree-lined road; we even walked into the bush but we couldn't find the perfect single tree. Some trees looked wonderful covered with snow but when the snow was removed, so was their beauty. Sometimes in the Cariboo we would tie two small trees together to make one bushy tree. We might have to do that today.

We had just about given up on finding a tree. There was an entire forest of trees and not one perfect Christmas tree? As we neared the house I spotted a nice looking tree. It was small, it was bushy and near the road, however, it was still covered with snow. I slowed down to get a better look. At that moment Tasha spotted what she thought was the perfect tree on the opposite side of the road. "We want one," she shouted as she opened the door and scurried up the packed snow bank, "like this." As she reached out to show me the tree she tumbled headfirst over the packed snow bank into the freshly fallen, waist deep, powder snow.

In the end the perfect tree was found almost where we started the search at the end of the road. It was the perfect tree. It was the perfect how tall and the perfect how bushy without snow. I suppose we just needed an adventure.

NIGHT SEARCH

Ryan was always an extreme adventurer. Any activity that would cause my heart to be in my throat would be his first choice. I was very happy when he met his friend Boyd who loved fishing and aroused Ryan's interest. Fishing is a relaxing sport. There are no broken bones attributed to fishing. There is no loud cheering crowd. It is not a crazed competition of the most agile. Fishing is just relaxing and waiting for a bite. Or is it?

Ryan had broken his wrist playing soccer. There was not much that he could do with a broken wrist trapped in a heavy plaster cast. He was feeling very frustrated. It seemed that his life was completely changed because of one broken bone.

He wanted to go fishing at Duggan Lake which was about ten minutes cross-country on his motorbike, but how could he get there with a broken wrist? Riding his motorbike would be a thrash because the broken wrist extended on down to the clutch hand, not to mention the rough cross-country terrain he would have to maneuver. He got his motorbike out and had a few tries but it was impossible. He was unable to manipulate the clutch with the cast on his arm. Ryan is very determined and if there were a way to be found, he would be just the one to find it.

In the early afternoon I noticed him packing his fishing gear onto the motorbike. He waved goodbye and shouted "see you soon!" as he rode toward the five-mile hay field and out of sight. I worried about Ryan on his bike in the woods alone with a broken wrist but he had to make his own decisions.

I had my agenda so I wasn't noticing that the time was passing fast. When I looked at my watch it was already ten pm. Where could he be, I wondered? I hope that he hasn't had an accident in the woods! By eleven pm I was frantic. It was now pitch dark and still there was no sign of my Ryan. I listened for the sound of an approaching motor bike from the woods.

I decided that I would have to go look for him. He must be hurt to be this late. I got my motorbike out, gassed it up, opened the gate and I was on my way. I knew the trail he would take to the lake. If I stayed on the trail I should have no problem. As I passed through the rail gate I looked back for the last time. I really was riding out into the night alone.

I was very afraid but at this moment my need to find my Ryan was much greater than my fear of the dark or for my own safety. I didn't look back as I entered the woods. I was going at a pretty good clip for me, as fast as I could go on a rutted muddy logging road in the night. Suddenly I felt brave; I could conquer the world if I had to. No wild animals would dare be so foolish as to get in the way in my present state of mind.

Oh-my-gosh! There are lights coming up from behind me. Even worse than wild animals, hunters had found me alone in the woods and at night. I screamed but I couldn't even hear myself over the roar of the bikes. The lights were gaining on me. I was going as fast as I could but they kept gaining on me. At last the other bike was by my side and I could hear Ryan's voice calling to me.

Ryan had arrived home just in time to see my tail lights disappear into the woods. He knew that it would be me out looking for him so he came out to stop me. I was so happy to see my Ryan all in one piece. I was also annoyed that he allowed me to be so frightened I would venture out in the pitch dark to find him, risking my own life.

Yes, Ryan was born an extreme adventurer. He wouldn't allow a broken bone or a cast cheat him out of a day of fishing or me out of a night search.

THE CENTENARIAN

I worked for many years as a home support worker in the Central Cariboo area of BC. I would visit several clients in a day. Doing for them the things they couldn't do for themselves; taking from them any life-stories they cared to share. Sometimes when their usual caregivers went away, I would do respite care which was around-the-clock care in their home.

I was doing respite care with Elsie, the one hundred year old daughter of a Kamloops area pioneer. She was a very active woman with all her faculties intact. She had been a nurse in her younger days. Elsie loved to learn and do new things and she was very exciting to be around. She loved to talk about the olden days but she was equally as interested in what was going on today. Nothing thrilled her more than to learn something new.

I took my niece to visit Elsie because she knew a lot about Wilfrid Laurier, former Prime Minister of Canada from 1896 to 1911, about whom Angela was doing a report. Angela was fascinated by Elsie and her vast knowledge. She wanted to take Elsie to school for Show and Tell. Elsie thought going to school was a great idea and she was game. She was willing to do anything that was exciting.

On one of my days with Elsie, I allowed my son to use my car to go to Williams Lake. Elsie had an appointment at one o'clock that same day and Ryan knew to be back by noon. He had come cross-country on his motor bike to get the car and he parked his bike in front of the house.

Sometime before noon Elsie asked, "Do you think that Ryan will be back in time for my appointment?" As she spoke, she glanced out the window where she saw the motor bike parked. "It won't matter," she said, "we could just go to Williams Lake on that motor bike."

Elsie was in possession of all her faculties. She was most exciting to spend time with. At one hundred years of age she was a treasure house of information and generous in sharing it. The most common thing she could be heard saying was, "Can you even imagine living a hundred years never knowing this or never trying that. "

SAVED BY THE WALL

In the summer of 1992, I was fed up with the shallow clothes closet in my bedroom. When the length of the hanger exceeds the depth of the closet, well, you can see my dilemma.

Having examined the wall from both sides, I noticed that the wallboard of the closet was fireproof and it was fifteen inches away from the chimney. The hallway wallboard, also fireproof, was only about four inches away from the chimney so I decided to make some structural changes. I would only have to remove the nails holding the back closet wall, move the wall back about ten inches and replace the nails. It appeared to be a simple straightforward job. I estimated that this job should take me an hour or two. The fine finishing later may be more time-consuming.

Larry went to work in Mackenzie; he would be away flying with forestry four to six weeks doing controlled burns. This was the right time to start just in case it took me longer than my estimated time. I had a bad habit of not factoring in all the miscellaneous things that could and often did happen during my major home renovation projects. I gathered together the various tools I would need and made my way upstairs to the spare bedroom.

The project seemed to be going along well; nowhere near as tough as I'd anticipated. I may not even need all the time I allotted myself. Only one nail that I could see remained. That last nail was high up on the back side of the closet wall. I went into the bathroom in the spare bedroom where I was stretched snugly between the chimney and the back of the closet wall in order to pull that one remaining nail out. It was difficult getting the hammer claws around the last nail using my less than co-operative left hand. I pushed myself farther into that crevice and at last I could reach with my right hand. The hammer claws were firm around the head of that nail. I had a tight grip with my right hand and I gave a hard pull loosening the nail. Just then the floor beneath my feet gave way and I was dangling through the floor between the closet wall and the chimney. I moved my feet trying to get a grip on solid floor and as I found some, that floor slipped away also.

I was unable to look down to see what was happening at my feet, because of my position. My right arm was above my head holding the hammer that was hooked on the last nail. My left arm was above my head pushed hard against the hallway wall because I was falling through the floor. I couldn't turn my head for the spikes sticking out the back of the closet wall and jagged strips of metal sticking out of the chimney.

I knew I was in deep trouble; no one would be coming to look for me. I was quite sure that I would die where I was in the wall. By the time that Larry came home six weeks from now I would be decomposing in the wall, my feet dripping down onto the living room carpet below.

I was in the habit of writing a note and drawing a map then leaving them on the kitchen table if I was going off into the woods; if a rescuer happened by, there would at least be a clue as to my whereabouts. I didn't think all that would be necessary to make a trip to the spare bedroom.

Things had changed considerably. I had worked so hard to get that last nail out and now I wanted it to hold fast. There was no point in shouting; the neighbors were over a kilometer away cross-country and I was inside the wall. I struggled but I couldn't find solid footing nor could I move; yet I felt sure that I could slide right through that hole in the floor. I cried hysterically as I thought of dying alone between the wall and the chimney. All that got me was a wet face, a runny nose that made me want to sneeze and that I couldn't even wipe. I continued to struggle.

Why did I always do this to myself? Why did I start big projects when I was alone by myself with no one? My feet were dangling through the floor. My body was bleeding and crisp from being scratched on the nails and the metal strips which also had a tight grip on my long hair. I knew that no one would even look for me for a minimum of four weeks and likely six. Anyway, who would think to look for me in the wall?

I struggled again to get one of my toes up on to the bottom board of the closet wall. I would still be stuck but at least I wouldn't be falling through the floor. Hours passed, I was getting tired. I begged God to help me get out of this mess. I suppose that I still had a lesson to learn because help was not forthcoming. I knew that I would surely die right here where I was.

After much searching with a single toe, I was able to wiggle one big toe onto something that felt secure. Suddenly my desire to escape overcame the fear of falling through the floor. I put pressure on that board with one toe. It seemed solid. I managed to move that big toe to a more secure-feeling place on a board. Then I put some more toes up.

Well, I wasn't going to fall through the floor now. I twisted and wiggled until I could get my second big toe up on the board and then my entire second foot. My clothing and my hair were caught on nails and jagged metal strips and this was preventing me from pushing myself up. Where are the scissors when you need them? My arms and my hands were numb from being over my head for hours. I feared that the hammer I held might fall those eighteen inches from my hand and onto my head. I forced myself up, tearing my shirt, pulling my hair out by the roots and cutting my skin. I was on solid ground now! I would escape!

When at last I was free of my possible upright tomb, I thanked God for saving my life. I examined the falling floor or should I say the hole in the floor to find that those two fallen pieces were simply set in place. There was nothing to actually hold them where they were set. I suppose that if no one chose to move the wall they would have been fine as they were for a hundred years. They would not ever have been walked on or touched for any reason.

Later that day, knowing the hazards I faced and of course after the fact, I got on with the project of getting that nail out and moving the wall.

Now you ask, was being able to hang my clothes in my closet worth all that? Yes, you bet it was!

TREASURES

I so wanted a deer skull with the antlers attached to decorate my flower garden on the north side of the house. Imagine how thrilled I was when I got one deer head from a friend and one from a neighbor. There was just one itsy-bitsy problem with these skulls; they were fresh off deer that had been shot the previous week. I was only a wanna-be country girl, so there was a lot about the country that I didn't know yet. I was sure that I would have to put the skulls out of reach of coyote, fox, wolf and cougar while they spent time drying.

I really had no place to keep them. I did, however, live next to a hay field with a creek running through it. There were a lot of trees along the creek. It would be a great hiding place to hang the heads until they were clean.

It was late fall during hunting season when I was given the deer heads. We were having an El Nino kind of winter in 1997-1998 so there was very little snow in the Cariboo. I climbed through the barbed wire fence with my two deer heads; rope, spikes, hammer and a pocket knife and all the tools I thought I might need. I made my way to the perfect hiding place across the hay field into the woods along the creek. I found a lot of tall trees there but how was I going to get the deer heads way up there? The branches started more than half way up on most of those tall thin poplars, better known to residents as Cariboo Palm trees.

I climbed onto a log that had floated down the creek during the spring flood last year and pounded several spikes into the tree as high up as I could reach. I tied rope onto the spikes and commenced tying the deer heads up there one at a time. Wrapping the rope around the jaw, then the spike, then the antlers, then the spike they appeared to be up there very securely. I was pleased that I was able to get up so high in the trees. When I stepped down and back it didn't look very high at all. When I climbed up the bank they seemed to be hanging rather low, lower than the bank in fact. I worried a lot about that.

I was so pleased that we were having an El Nino winter with hardly any snow. If snow had fallen and frosted over, any creatures would have been able to walk on the top of the snow and make quick work of my deer skulls.

I would walk across the frozen field every once in a while to check their progress but it's like watching a tea kettle boil. Nothing really happened in that first year. Now a second year has passed and I still don't know how old I'll be when they are clean and finally ready to put in the garden. They seemed to be drying out rather than getting cleaned.

I was getting tired of waiting so I went to the woods in the autumn and took those silly heads down. I took them home and planted them in the garden leaving only the antlers above ground. I was happy to at least have the antlers in my garden, although wild creatures kept pulling them out of the ground.

That year I planned to move to Calgary and I decided to give the antlered skulls away to my country friend Vona.

In the spring when I was ready to move to Calgary, I dug up the skulls to find that they were perfect and perfectly clean treasures. It was the natural way of cleaning a skull; it only took a few months as opposed to a few years and a lot of hard work on the part of this city slicker-cum-country girl.

BLACK AS NIGHT

I was house-sitting in Miocene when my friend Paul came from Vancouver to visit. Paul loves a good adventure and perhaps that's why we came to meet. We talked for hours when he arrived and when it got dark out we decided to go out for a walk. We have always enjoyed a long slow walk in the dark. On a short leash we took along the adult bull mastiff dog that only understands Japanese. My Japanese was and still is non-existent so I depended on specific tugs on the leash to issue my commands.

There was no moon or stars in the sky to guide us or to light our way. As we walked away from the porch light we realized how very dark it was. We held hands because we couldn't even see one another. We were walking along the highway. The only way to know that we were still on the side of the road was to have one of us walk on the pavement and the other walk on the gravel.

Now and then a vehicle would drive by and give us some light so we could see where we were. When it passed we were blinded. A short distance along we turned off the highway onto Wiggins Road. It's the old highway that runs parallel to Horsefly Road, the present highway. Eventually Wiggins Road turned and came out to the Horsefly Road again. This is the round trip that we usually took when

Paul came to visit, although most often through fields and woods in the daylight.

We could hear noises in the woods around us. We talked loud and laughed a lot to keep our spirits light and in hopes of warding off any scary animals. We did pass a few houses on our journey but the lights were dim and distant, however, the farm dogs found it necessary to bark and snarl at the gates.

As we turned to go back out to the highway we had to cross over a metal cattle guard. It was dangerous to walk over it in the daytime and tonight we couldn't even see it. The dog was not happy about the cattle guard or Texas gate as some farmers call it, but fortunately he had been over it many times and knew what was expected. I gave him all the lead possible.

We could hear animals in the hay field beside us and we hoped that they were cows but we picked up speed anyway. When we approached the second cattle guard we knew that we were very near the highway again. We crossed that second cattle guard carefully, one pipe at a time. When we got to the opposite side we waited for a vehicle to come by so we could find our way safely across the highway.

Soon we were on our way back to the house, one of us on the pavement and one on the gravel. After all that time out in the dark our eyes never did adjust to the darkness. As we neared the house the porch light bade us welcome. We three had survived our trip in the pitch-darkness.

CRUISING DOWN THE CHILCO

In 1993 I met Ruby Tufts a delightful and elegant lady of eighty years. Though there was a huge gap in our age we had a great deal in common. We were both adventure seekers and if no adventure presented itself we were not above searching one out. We talked about living on the edge, the things that we had done in our lives and the things that we had always wanted to do. We learned that we were both seeking the excitement and adventure of whitewater rafting. We talked about going on a rafting trip together in the future. Rafting would mean a trip to Kamloops or Golden because there was no rafting around the Cariboo Chilcotin area.

One day while reading the local newspaper we saw an advertisement for Chilco River Expeditions, rafting on the Chilco River. It sounded like it was near by; it must be in the Chilcotin area with a name like that. We would have to make inquires about it.

Wow, imagine! Rafting in our own area! We'd have to think about it more seriously. That year we didn't get around to checking it out. Perhaps we weren't as brave as we thought we were! We talked about it often enough! I worried about Ruby because she was over eighty three years by then. She said that my worry was just foolishness;

she was perfectly capable. There was no doubt that she was up to the challenge. Soon it was late August; it was getting cold and too late in the year for us to go. Maybe next year we'd do it!

It was spring 1998 when once again we saw that advertisement luring us to the river. We called to see if this company would be willing to take Ruby rafting. There may be concerns about her age. To our surprise and pleasure Murphy said yes, he would live on the edge and he would be pleased to take Ruby on a one-day rafting trip. Ruby would be the oldest rafter he had taken out to date. She was now eighty-four years old.

We made our reservation for mid-July. Ruby started exercising to be in shape for the wild and crazy adventure. When mid-July arrived our trip was cancelled so we re-booked for the next weekend. We had to be at the Manor in Riske Creek at eight in the morning to meet the bus. I met Ruby at her place at about seven and we went speeding up highway twenty. It was a long drive out to the Manor. We had to drive up the steep twisted Sheep Creek Hill but soon we were passing the road marking yellow (highway centre line paint) buildings of Riske Creek.

As we reached the Manor we found many young excited rafters waiting. Even being thirty years younger than Ruby I felt old in this group. Soon the bus arrived with the rest of the rafters. We all signed waivers paid our fees and climbed on the bus that was humming with excitement. We were told about the accident that had injured two of our guides. It had not been a rafting accident but I started to have second thoughts about our safety. Ruby was still game. Concerned about being shown up by a senior citizen I shut my mouth.

The bus traveled on highway twenty to Lee's Corner at Hanceville. We stopped there to stock up on rafting snacks and plastic bags to wrap handbags and cameras. Next we made our way down to the river where the rafts were in the water waiting for us to board. This was our last chance to change our minds. Ok, we're going! We slipped on our life jackets, had a picture taken with Murphy and made our way down to the rivers edge and the rafts.

Ruby and I boarded the vessel. It was unnerving to discover that there were no seats. Sitting comfortably is a function carried out only by the guide who runs the long oars during the excursion! Our position choices would be astride the round edge of the raft, one foot in the cold river and one foot in the cold water on the floor of the raft or standing at the back leaning into the inside edge of the raft. We made our choices and prepared to launch.

I glanced at the water and my eyes became riveted there. The movement of the water mesmerized me and my stomach began to turn. I knew that I wouldn't be able to do this. I was going to be sick. The very perceptive and water-smart guide saw what was happening to me. He immediately directed me to focus on the horizon rather than the water. I felt better at once.

It was here that we were given our rafting instructions, Row! Left! Right! Stop! Hang on to your paddle! There may have been more instructions but I thought that there were already far too many. At last the rafts loaded, all passengers equipped with paddles, the guides aboard each raft, we pushed off from the security of shore.

My heart danced with the mixture of excitement and fear that I was feeling. It wasn't long until we challenged our first white water. Everyone was screaming but those who got wet screamed the loudest by far. It seemed to me that our handsome bronzed guide could manipulate the raft with those long oars so that chosen people would get wet and now it was our turn. I was concerned for Ruby but she was having the time of her life. She looked like a seasoned pro, drenched to the skin and screaming along with all the rest. It wasn't long until everyone aboard was soaked to the skin, including myself.

When we started out at about nine thirty that morning the water seemed cold; now that we were wet through it seemed quite comfortable. It was a wonderful warm day. It was not hot enough to burn the skin, yet warm enough to be very comfortable rafting.

We came to an island in the river where we beached our raft and people dispersed in all directions at once. It didn't take long to figure out that this was a potty break and we too must find the tallest, widest weed to hide behind as we went about the business of fertilizing the land. With everyone relieved we re-boarded our raft and soon were careening out to white water once again.

Sometimes we floated gently and slowly along the mighty Chilco River. We admired the scenery, the rock formations created by time and weather; we also enjoyed the opposite view from the bottom of the canyon reserved for rafters. We were among the privileged few to have seen that particular view. We drifted near the shore as we slipped around a bend. There, just above us, in a standing dead tree sat a majestic Bald Eagle family surveying their hunting grounds. The eagles looked down and watched as the noisy intruders passed by.

It was lunchtime and everyone was feeling the pangs of hunger as we beached our raft and commenced to disembark a second time. Quickly the raft was emptied of its passengers and its contents. Everyone seemed busy. Some people built a fire, others helped set up the lunch table, some people just looked for a place to sit and relax. I found a fallen tree for Ruby to sit on. It wasn't exactly as high or as straight as it needed to be but oh well, this was the wilderness and we made do. When lunch was ready to be served there was a wasp infestation attracted by the delicious aromas. Every wasp resented the fact that we wanted a taste of our gourmet lunch. I got lunch ready for Ruby and brought it to her. The wasps were already sharing her food. She suffered a sting to her lip as she tried to get a morsel of her lunch. I didn't want a sting because of severe sting allergies so I chose not to eat. It was a lovely gourmet lunch but it seemed that everyone was happy to lend a hand cleaning up and packing up so we could leave that wasp-infested location.

As we boarded the raft for the last time some of us changed positions. Ruby moved to the opposite side of the raft which she found to be much more comfortable for her. I moved up to the front to get a different experience. Since our lunch break it seemed that there was more white water than before and the water seemed faster. We spent a lot of time paddling. Left, left, left, stop, right, right, harder!

I barely recognized Farwell Canyon; I had never seen it from this particular angle before. Right, right, right! We were pulling in to shore in that rough water. People were leaping out of the raft and helping to pull it to shore. Now it was my turn to leap out. I hated to leave Ruby on the raft when I was off but quickly two strong young men lifted her to the shore. We took a moment to get our land legs and we started walking along the beach and up the bank. We had survived the whitewater of the mighty Chilco.

The sun was setting now; the day was cooling off. A fire was blazing in preparation for the evening steak bar-b-que. Tents were being assembled, wet clothing hung to dry and people warmed up around the fire. We were as wet as could be and had no change of clothes with us. We warmed up in Murphy's vehicle then we purchased some souvenir T-shirts that read, "Chilco River Expeditions, The Essence of Adventure." This was an accurate description of our trip. The shirts were much too big, but oh well, they were warm and dry! We changed into those shirts and felt warmer straight away.

Soon we were leaving the rafting party. We'd had such a fun day and were regretting our decision to take the one-day rather than the overnight trip. My sore throat told me that I had screamed at least three times, once from take off to potty break, once from potty break to lunch stop and once from lunch stop to Farwell Canyon.

Even with a huge gap in our ages we had a great deal in common. We were both adventure seekers; we liked to live on the edge. Today we lived our dream of whitewater rafting as we went cruising down the mighty Chilco River.

THE RECOVERY ROOM

I was visiting with Gertie, at the High-Way Trailer Park. Gertie had a lovely chair that needed some TLC. As I looked at the chair I thought I could recover it for her in no time at all. I was having ten months off work so I certainly would have the time. I asked if I could do it for her and she was thrilled to let me. Arnold carried the chair to my house so that I could get started.

Time passed and somehow I couldn't get going. I decided that maybe I really didn't want to do it. It would be more work than anticipated. It had been my idea; I should get on with it! I kept the chair in my way so I wouldn't forget about it. It was in the middle of the living room or at the end of my bed so I had to make a great effort to avoid it. Still I couldn't get going. Time was passing; it had been months now. I had everything that I needed; why couldn't I get going? It was obvious now that it would take a lot longer. I stopped talking about it; I did however, continue to walk around the chair. I didn't dare put it out of sight now that I was feeling so apathetic about it. Gertie never did ask about the chair, she didn't want to rush me.

Well, now a year had passed and I was plenty tired of avoiding that chair. Today is the day. Whatever else may occur today this chair would be done before the sun went down. I sat on the floor in front of the dreaded chair as I tried to recall the original plan for it. I gathered together all the necessary tools, scissors, tacks, fabric, hammer, needle, thread and stapler. I was ready; I vowed to stay in this spot on the floor until the chair was done. I spread the fabric on the floor where I started cutting patterns, tearing strips for the ruffle and stapling. It all went together like magic; one pleasing step after another.

In no time the chair was finished and it looked like new. My neighbor was impressed and pleased to have her chair back. In the end, once I applied myself, the job only took two hours. OK! OK! It took exactly one year and two hours.

GATHERING WINTER WOOD

We always knew that we would have to gather wood for the winter. Our log home was heated with wood. I, in particular, liked to see enough wood cut and stacked in the yard to last three years prior to the first snowfall or cold weather. It's not that I expected this work to be done for me. I was out there working just as hard and getting just as dirty as the next guy.

All year long as I drove our road, I always had my eye open for dead standing or dead fallen trees. I was looking for the specific trees that were just the right size for me to carry when they were cut because I only wanted to do the work once. No chopping for me. I also wanted to know that when Larry said, "Let's go for wood," I would be able to point out enough dead wood to make the day-trip worthwhile.

When we planned to go out gathering winter wood we prepared all our chainsaws in advance. We'd sharpen and tighten the chains and fill the oil. We'd bring along files for touch-ups, extra oil and plenty of gas to run the saws. Knowing we'd be gone for the day, we also brought food and refreshments. We carried a bottle of mosquito repellant and a variety of jackets. Our big dog Sparky usually spent the day with us. It was his rare opportunity to run freely in the woods away from home. It was always a fun family day trip when we went out to gather wood.

Each person on the team had his job. One person cut the tree down insuring that it fell in the right direction. We didn't want to walk one inch further than necessary. One person de-limbed the tree and cut it into lengths. Another person dragged the logs to the wagon and loaded them. It was everyone's job to keep an eye on the dog and the falling trees, shouting "Timber" each time one fell.

Unless we recruited Harold and his horses to tow the logs out of the woods, we would not go more than a few feet off the road. We would tow the wagon behind the old Scout loading it up as the trees came down and were cut to length. I liked to go in the summer or the fall to get wood because of my winter wood phobia.

Conrad liked his wood to warm him twice; once while cutting it and again when burning it in his stove. He would just go out when he was out of wood in the winter. I was horrified by the prospect of being out of wood in the winter. I needed to see lots of cut wood piled neatly in the yard near the house prior to the first cold weather or snow. I was on about it all the time to the point of being annoying. I didn't mind going logging in the winter as long as it was for someone else.

In winter we would bunch the logs, chain them together and tow them home using the cat or the tractor. Somehow the wood always made it home where it was always cut to length and stacked before the day was over. As we created piles of sawdust we would move the wagon and burn the sawdust to either keep the mosquitoes away in summer or to keep us warm in winter.

When wood is your only source of winter heat, especially if you have a phobia such as mine, dead standing wood and gathering winter wood is first and foremost on your mind all year long.